DREAMS FROM NEPAL

The Emotional Story of a Twelve-Year-Old Nepali Boy

By Bikul Koirala

Dreams from Nepal by Bikul Koirala

www.bikul.net

© 2017 Bikul Koirala

All rights reserved. No portion of this book may be reproduced in any form without permission from the author, except as permitted by U.S. copyright law. For permissions contact:

bikul@kduoapps.com

Edited by Coral Coons

ISBN: 9781549508608

Contents

Introduction & Acknowledgement iii
1 Luxury 1
2 The Crossroads 9
3 The Land Rover 16
4 A New Light 23
5 Badminton 28
6 Empty Vessel 35
7 Mount Everest 41
8 Birthday Cake 46
9 Penance 53
10 A Mother's Touch 60
11 House Boy 72
12 Home 82
13 The Gift 90
14 Egypt 100
15 Priya 107
16 The Tapestry 117
17 Departure 123
18 Big News 129
19 Good Fortune 133
20 The Middle Way 139
21 Loyalty 144
Glossary .... a
About the Author c

Introduction & Acknowledgement

This book has been in my mind for almost ten years now. I have always found reasons to not write this book, but I have run out of excuses. So, here it is – my debut novel.

This book is very much a work of fiction, but there are stories close to me that have made it into the book in one form or another. You will not have to look far or hard to find real-life stories similar to this in the villages of Nepal. Economically-strained parents are forced to make difficult choices every day.

This journey through Ram's life is an emotional story. It is a story of love and sacrifice. It is a story of culture and society. It is a story of a young boy's determination and perseverance. It is a story of life!

This book would not have come to fruition without the support of my family. To my parents, Madan and Bidya Koirala, your creative writing motivated me throughout my childhood. To the love of my life, Anisa, you are my rock! You have supported me through every crazy dream I wanted to chase. Bobo, our little pup, deserves equal thanks for getting me out of my chair for play time and just being the best friend a man could ask for.

I'd love to hear from you. Thanks for all your support.

Love,

Bikul Koirala

August 1, 2017

1.

Luxury

Ram had his eyes fixed on the television set for almost ten minutes now. His eyes sparkled as he wondered how all those people fit in that little box. He routinely dreamed of what it would be like to have one of those in their own home. More than the TV itself, he wondered about the lives of people who were in it.

It was just last year that he saw a TV for the first time. Baba had taken him to a neighborhood village for a carnival, where he first saw the magical box. Ram could not believe his eyes as he stared at that little black box with people inside it – people that moved and talked and laughed. He kept looking behind the box to see where all those people were. All Ram wanted to do was sit in front of it and watch and listen to the happy, colorful world of the people inside.

Ram had one pair of clothes that he wore most times. His mother had patched it up in several places. The people in the TV changed into different clothes and ate portions of food he could only imagine. He wanted to live a life like theirs. He wanted to wear clothes like the people on TV did. He wanted to see the places that he saw in that box.

He was deep in his dream world when he heard someone calling his name.

"Ram!" yelled a familiar voice. "We have to finish up the shopping and start heading back to the village before it gets dark."

Ram recognized his father's soft yet stern voice. No matter how lost he was in his dreams, he knew not to ignore Baba. Everyone in the village called their father Ba or Buwa, but Ram never grew out of his childhood habit of calling his father Baba. There was a sense of security he felt when he heard the word. It was like his own special name for his father. He felt like the word embodied his love for his father better than any other.

Ram's life was not the same as a typical twelve-year-old kid's. Ram and his family lived in a small, two-room mud hut in the village of Chandisthan, located at the foothills of the Annapurna Mountains, with the Himalayas just behind it. Most houses in Ram's village were like his — mud with a bamboo roof. Some were painted in bright colors, but most had shades of orange, brown, or red from the mud. It was a modest place to live, but he and his family were modest people.

He went to school for two years some time back, but had to stay home and help Baba after his youngest brother was born. Ram had a large family, but not the largest in their village. He had two brothers and two sisters, all four of them younger than him and each one barely a year and a half apart.

Ram just turned twelve last month. No one remembered his actual birthday. There was no party or elaborate birthday celebration. There was no cake, and certainly no presents. Ama and Baba gave him their blessings and Ama made him his favorite food: rice pudding. Ram loved the rice pudding Ama made. The thick mixture of rice and milk with sprinkles of cashew and raisins and a subtle hint of cardamom and clove was so rich in flavor that he could almost taste it as soon as he laid his eye on it. It had to be a special occasion in Ram's household to justify delicacies like rice pudding or meat.

Ama spent most of her days fetching water and firewood, cooking, cleaning and taking care of the kids. Most hours of the day, she was hunched over the wood stove, baby on her back, coughing, trying to keep the fire going. She looked so small from afar that it was almost difficult to see her in the dark kitchen.

Ama was barely five feet tall and weighed less than one hundred pounds. Ram often watched in disbelief as his mom returned from her morning trip to the nearby woods with a large load of firewood on her back and her baby son strapped to her front. It looked like the <u>doko</u> of firewood she carried on her back weighed as much as her. He could not understand how she had the strength to wake up before dawn and go through the motions of the day.

Regardless of how tired she would be by the time she got back home, he could count on her to smile at him as she put her load down at the front porch. He would always go running to her with a glass of cold water to help her cool down. He would then give her an update on how his younger siblings were doing and when Baba expected to be back for lunch. She loved this about Ram. He was only twelve, but he behaved like an adult. He did not care to run around the village, playing and chasing animals. He preferred to stay at home and help his parents keep an eye on his younger siblings. At least, even if he wanted to be out playing, he was extremely talented at hiding it.

Baba called him again, so Ram turned away from the television and dutifully followed him through the market. He had been looking forward to their annual trip to the market all year; the TV could wait a while longer.

The closest town to his own was Pokhara, a popular tourist mecca for Westerners coming to trek into the Annapurnas. This was where the market was located. There was a vibrant main thoroughfare off the quieter roads that wound around and down to Phewa Lake. On a calm day, Phewa reflected the majestic peak of Mount Machhapuchhre, as well as other mountains in the Annapurna and Dhualagiri Ranges.

The peaks were not new to ram, as having them right in his backyard made them familiar. What made the trip special and what made him look forward to the coveted excursions was a sense of adventure. It was as far as he had ever been from where he grew up, but to Ram, it seemed like another world. Second only to his home village, Pokhara was Ram's favorite place to be.

Together, he and Baba strolled through the market. Stores lined the streets, offering everything imaginable in the way of household goods. Every opportunity Ram got, he tried to talk to the tourists with a big smile on his face. He ran up to them, saying "Hello, Sir" or "Namaste, Miss". He wanted to learn more about their lives and their countries. Every once in a while, a tourist would sit down with him at the tea shop and show him pictures of their country on their phones. Many of them seemed to live like the people in the TV did – like he wanted to. He felt excitement and curiosity as he imagined himself in those places.

There were always tourists, both national and international, around the lake. Ram loved telling the tourists how Machapuchhre was a sacred mountain and no one had ever conquered it. He displayed pride in being able to share local knowledge that the tourists might not be aware of. Ram also loved to accompany his father on their trips to Pokhara, much like this one. He tagged along behind him as he haggled with merchants along the bustling street. There were so many fascinating things to see.

Ram's father never purchased more than the most meager of offerings, but the variety of shiny, strange-looking items kept Ram's eyes wide open and entertained him as they walked along. Also, navigating the regular assortment of cattle that wandered about and took up space for mid-day naps was part of the adventure. A combination of the religions that swirled through this part of the country provided a special approval of the animals, and so they were accepted as part of the surroundings.

The air was fresh and crisp outside, as it always was in the mountain villages. The land in this high altitude was not always fertile and the weather was never predictable, but Ram loved it anyway. He took a breath of the cool mountain air and smiled, lost in thought as they made their way through the village streets.

The sound of the farmers making their way to the market place down the road from Chandisthan brought Ram back to reality. The louder-than-normal clatter of carts and oxen and conversations of the men was a bit more frenzied around this time of the year. Each farmer knew that winter would soon be upon them. They wanted to conclude the growing season with a flourish; they knew whatever they traded in the next month or so would have to sustain them until the spring.

Despite this, Ram's family somehow managed to produce barely enough crops to get them through the unrelenting cold and snow of the winter. Every year, Baba worried if they were going to have enough food to last until next harvest. All they could grow in this altitude was potatoes and barley, but this family knew how to make it work with what they had. He carefully rationed and stored the harvests and traded in the market for other essentials.

One thing that Ram knew was that, despite how it might look to an outsider, his life was good. At least that was how he saw it. Not everyone in the village was as fortunate as Ram and his parents. Ram and his family had their own land they could farm on and had been lucky to have good crops years in a row. Less than half of the village had this luxury. His father often stepped in to offer help when supplies and food ran short for others in the winter. Ram supposed that some might see this as foolish and risky, but they always seemed to get by somehow. It was a lesson he took to heart early in his life, and he looked up to his father and his altruistic efforts.

Based on this, Ram began and ended each day in prayer and gratitude for what he and his family had. He never thought of being in need or of living in a sense of scarcity, even though his friends in Chandisthan often teased him for his practices. That was not to say that Ram wanted to continue as his parents lived. They always provided for him, and Ram could never remember a time where he was ever truly wanting for basic necessities or had gone hungry.

He did, though, see how they struggled and worked themselves to fatigue each day to make sure this was the case. On trips outside of Chandisthan, Ram was quick to notice how others were thriving, rather than just getting by. He had even heard of people who had the magical black boxes in their home. He did not view them with envy or jealousy, though. Rather, Ram looked up to these people, wanting to be like them when he grew up. He had no idea what it was that they did that allowed them this level of success over mere survival. But he was curious, and when daydreaming during his chores at home, he imagined big things for himself. He had wanted so much more out of his life, for himself, his parents, and his own family one day.

Ram had learned one thing as he had grown up from his observations: it would take a good education to make this leap of ambition. He had no idea how that was going to happen, as his parents had no money for such an endeavor. With extra mouths to feed at home, he knew that his chances of going back to school were slim to none. On his own, Ram tried to learn all he could about any topic available to him. *It might not be a formal education*, he thought, *but every little bit helps*. Ram never let any opportunity pass him by.

Today, the opportunity he most looked forward to was spending time at the lake with Baba. After a day on the street, Ram and his father often retreated from the heat of the day to seek refuge in the tree-lined roads near the lake. Ram would watch with great interest as tourists gorged on the platters of fish delicacies from the lake. Unfortunately, his family's income would not allow for such luxuries.

He would usually split one of the large mango or banana lassis – which the local cafés were famous for – with his father as they rested before the return trip home. He was always grateful for these moments. Simply getting out and away from his routine life in Chandisthan was enough. Plus, he loved this time alone with his father.

Then, on the long journey home from Pokhara, Ram and his father would have long conversations about a wide range of topics. He loved asking his father about how the place was when he was a young boy himself. Baba would often tell him stories about the time he went to the capital, like when there was a helicopter in village when the king visited. Ram loved listening to his father's stories and very often imagined himself in his father's place.

Today, though, none of this happened.

As they walked through the busy trading shops in town, Ram noticed a change in his father's behavior. He could not help but notice that on this particular trip, his father seemed to be doing more perusing than actual buying. It was not until the end of the afternoon, long after Ram had bid farewell to the tourists he had been speaking with, that

Baba finally stopped at one shop and made a few purchases. Ram watched in silent surprise as his father's satchel was filled with a small fraction of what he normally would have bought. There was something in his father's eyes that gave Ram concern, but he knew better than to ask, especially here in public.

Normally, his father laughed easily and joked with him constantly as they passed the time on the road. Today, though, his father was quite reserved and reticent. He tried to think if he had made any mistakes or got in some trouble otherwise. He could not think of anything – at least not anything to cause such relative quietness from his normally cheerful and talkative father. He could not recall any incident in the village or on the way that would have brought about such a situation. Perhaps he had spent too long in front of the TV, but his father would have said something if he had. He also knew very well that his father had no problem confronting him directly and immediately if something had displeased him.

They walked in silence. His father never seemed to take his eyes off the ground, as if he was in deep thought. Ram remained shielded from the specifics of the family's means of support. Even so, Ram had sensed that this year had likely not been as plentiful for them as past years. This was his father's responsibility, not Ram's. Baba had made this clear to the whole family on multiple occasions, so Ram just did what he was asked and otherwise kept his questions to himself. His father was not prone to anger or fits of temper, but was stern and demanding all the same.

Ram did not probe as they hurriedly left the market and began their journey home. He stared longingly in the direction of the lake as they went, but did not ask his father if they could stop there. He knew, somehow, that it was not going to happen.

Ram intervened only once as they made their way back, as whatever was distracting his father had made him oblivious to a large cow stretched across the walkway. Ram grabbed his father's arm right before he might have stumbled over the large animal, who was busy filling its empty stomach with cardboard debris from the ground.

He knew that, being a devout Hindu, his father would not be happy if he stepped on a cow. After all, they worshipped the cow as a form of a goddess. There was even a day during the Diwali festival dedicated to the worshipping of cows. This one day, everyone put flower garlands on the cows and gave them a variety of food to feast on. Then, the day after, things were back to normal. There was no concern about the cows laying on the street. No one cared enough to be nice to the stray cows. This had always bothered Ram, but today, he ignored his feelings. He was more concerned about his father.

His father bleated out a small and nearly inaudible reply of appreciation to Ram as they skirted the poor beast. This was yet another sign that something was not quite right.

They returned to the cart and Ram's father mounted the seat after carefully placing a very empty satchel in the back—at least relatively empty to what they usually came home with. There was only about five kilos of rice and a small bag of lentils. He saw another small bag of wheat and beans. There was no dried fish, which his father usually got for festivals. There were no varieties of lentils and there were no dried nuts. He could not imagine how his mother was going to make this food last.

Lost in his thoughts, Ram took his own seat and watched in disappointment and sadness as his father steered the cart back to the road for the trek home. There would be no side trip to Phewa Lake this year. And, of course, no lassi. Ram looked forward to this small treat all year. Yes, something was definitely not right.

On the slow trip home, Ram almost asked what might be wrong, but in the end, he held his tongue. All his life, he had known everything his father did had a well-founded reason. He was sure there was one behind this, as well. He glanced over on several occasions as they rode and there was a look of deep worry and almost anguish on his father's brow.

Whatever it was, Ram could easily put the annual treat of the lake and the lassi aside. They were both luxuries, anyway….

2.

The Crossroads

Ram carefully put the cart away, as was his responsibility upon the return of each trip to Pokhara. His father looked tired and downtrodden as he plodded away toward their small but well-maintained house. The sun was setting over the high peaks, casting long shadows down across the Newa Sekuwa Pass. It was late autumn, but to Ram, it felt like winter was just around the corner. Ram was feeling cold, even in his long-sleeve shirt and pants. The air seemed to have more of a bite to it already than Ram remembered from previous years.

As was often the case, Ram's highly active imagination took over. Staring up at the pass, he wished he could go up to Khudi Bazaar to observe and mingle with the trekkers as they stopped at the popular tourist attraction. The tourists would stop to acclimate or just rest before heading higher into the mountains. Ram was fascinated with all the apparent wealth of the visitors. He wanted to follow them and make small talk. Over the years, Ram had picked up enough English to be able to talk to them a bit. Maybe someone would even give him a trinket or treat from one of the small tea houses there. He loved meeting tourists; there was something about them that always attracted him. He did not understand why these tourists came from all over the world to his tiny village. Nevertheless, he appreciated them being there.

Ram was still looking up toward Khudi Bazaar, wondering what was happening there now, as he led the ox to its small and nearly collapsing shed. He snapped out of his trance as he looked back toward the house, seeing his mother gesturing for him to hurry up and come in. He had been so lost in his captivation with what might be going on up the track that he had not heard her calling.

As he entered the house, Ram's nostrils were filled with the aroma of his mother's lentil curry, one of his favorites. His father was already seated at the table, looking as discouraged and forlorn as he had on the trip back from Pokhara. His mother, a naturally quiet woman, smiled at him as she waited for Ram to take his seat.

He bowed his head while his father offered their traditional thanks for the meal. He waited eagerly as his mother moved to the table and spooned the thick, savory soup into bowls. Ram was anxious to begin, but he knew it was the household tradition to wait for his father to begin. He and his siblings could start after his father did. His mother would then eat last, after she served seconds to her husband and children. The woman who spent all her day preparing their food would only eat after everyone else left the kitchen.

Finally, Ram joined in as his father tasted from his hot bowl and offered the subtle yet well-known nod that signaled they could begin. Alongside the steaming bowls of the curry was a wooden plate piled with Tibetan bread. It was not one of Ram's favorites, but he was well aware how scarce the food of their meals could be, so he took a piece anyway. As was his way when this bread appeared, he doused it thoroughly in the lentil broth, knowing his mother's talents in the kitchen could make even this unappealing bread palatable. He made sure every inch of the bread was covered with the delicious lentil curry before he took a bite.

Normally, his father would have regaled his mother with the day's events, but whatever was on his mind had apparently carried over into the evening. Ram hazarded a sideways glance toward first his father, and then, his mother. His father, much like on the walk back to the cart from the shops in Pokhara, kept his gaze focused downward at his meal. Again, it was very unlike what Ram was accustomed to at mealtime. His mother caught his glance toward her and just smiled weakly back, indicating she had no idea what was wrong, but that whatever it was, he was not the cause.

After dinner, Ram planned to retreat to his small room to read his well-worn copy of *The Old Man and the Sea* by Ernest Hemingway, which he had gotten from an American hiker years ago. He must have read the thing a thousand times already, but he loved the story and it kept his English sharp. Even after all the times he had read it, there were still parts he could not follow, but each new time he hoped he would pick up some more of the language.

Before he had gone more than a few steps, his father beckoned both him and his mother to the main part of the house. They joined him beside the gentle fire that glowed in the room. Ram sat with his mother on some thick pillows that were next to the embers of the fireplace. His father stared into the small, flickering flames, but appeared to be almost looking *through* them. Ram and his mother both sat quietly and waited, knowing that whatever was on his mind would soon be revealed. This was his way.

With a long and exaggerated sigh, his father broke his apparent spell and looked at them, trying to smile. Ram knew immediately that his unsuccessful attempt at a simple smile was most likely the forbearer of grim news. Ram wondered what that news might be.

Ram's father was also barely five feet tall, with a bald head and a figure that was just skin and bones. The wrinkles in his skin were evidence of many years of working in the sun. He was in his early forties, but looked like he was in his sixties. The tough life in the foothills of the Himalayas had taken a toll on him. Nevertheless, he was a resilient man, so what news would be so dire as to weaken his resolve?

Baba took off his topi, wiped his face with it, then slowly sat down. It normally was not a problem for him to share his emotions in private with them. He was not an openly warm or overly expressive man, but they knew of his love for them. As worried as Ram was, this thought comforted him for a moment.

"Ram, my son. I would like to discuss something with you – and with your mother, as well."

To an outsider, this might have seemed odd, but it was not strange to Ram. Within their culture, it was well understood that the decisions surrounding a family in Chandisthan were always made at the sole discretion of the father. Ram wondered what his father's decision here would be.

"This past season, our crops did not do as well as in the past. It was a dry summer and the winds were very powerful, as you may remember. I have always counted on a surplus so that we could offer a hand to our neighbors when needed. This coming winter, that may not be possible."

Ram sighed inwardly with relief. He knew his father was generous and had a big heart. Apparently, this was what had been on his mind, causing him to act oddly. He hadn't done anything wrong, after all.

"In fact, we may have to go to others for help this winter. With the birth of your baby brother last year, what we can produce from our land is no longer enough to feed us all. I am ashamed as a father and husband to say this, but I cannot think of any way to support the family year-round."

That one hit Ram in the gut like a gunshot. Never in his life had this ever been the case. No wonder his father had been looking concerned all day. As Ram began thinking of ways he could help his father, Baba continued.

"There has been an offer for you, my son, that we are accepting. I have struggled with this for days now, but I think it will be best for us all."

Ram felt a chill despite the warm fire. But at the same time, he was curious as his father continued.

"There is nothing wrong with how we live, Ram. We are honest and hard-working, but sometimes, that is just not enough. This year has been one of those times. You are a good boy and I could have never asked for a more dedicated and responsible son. But I do not want to see you have to scrape and struggle all through your life as your mother and I have."

Ram felt suddenly conflicted. Wonder, anxiety, and curiosity flooded his mind.

"I see the wonder and excitement in your eyes each time we go to the market in Pokhara. You never say it, but I can see you want more from your life than to be a simple farmer and herder like me."

"Father, I never–"

His father now did manage a weak smile. He held up his hand gently to stop Ram from continuing.

"It's okay. There is nothing to be ashamed of in wanting more out of your life, son. I am proud that you have that ambition and curiosity of the world out there. This winter is going to be hard on us here. I do not want you to suffer from the shortcomings of the capriciousness of the gods. We have had many bountiful years here, and this year, we will be tested."

Suddenly, their dismal day made sense to Ram – the small purchases in Pokhara, not going to the lake, and coming directly home without an explanation. Now, he understood why, but he wasn't sure how he felt about it.

"For you to do more with your life, Ram, you will need a proper education. And, unfortunately, that cannot happen here. There are no schools in Chandisthan that can offer you what you need. Even if there were, we do not have the money to pay for it. To get the education you will need, you will need to go to a real city, with real schools. Kathmandu."

"Kathmandu?"

"Yes."

Ram was now utterly confused. If they had no money or the opportunity to send him to a school close by, then how was a school in Kathmandu even an option?

"But, father, how can we afford–"

His father again stopped him with the gentle raising of two fingers. He nodded and sighed again. It was one of the things that he both loved and found infuriating about Ram; his son was always thinking and asking questions about what he did not understand, but he was also often too abrupt and impatient with his inquiries.

"Which brings me to the offer I mentioned. There is a family in Kathmandu by the name of Kady. They live in a large and expansive place in Kathmandu and they need some help with household chores. The mother of the household cannot manage all the demands anymore while attending to her husband, two children, and other commitments that are required of her. They have offered to take you on in this capacity, which comes with the added bonus of allowing you to attend school. Part of the arrangement is that they will be responsible for your school expenses."

Ram fell silent. He had no idea what to say. He hated the thought of leaving his family and Chandisthan. But it was the chance to attend a real school. *I'll get an education at last! But in Kathmandu?*

He had never been there, but the thought of being alone in that huge city scared him. He had heard horror stories of what life in Kathmandu was like. He had no idea if they were true or not, but what he had heard was often appalling. He had spent his whole life in the safe and confined perimeter of Chandisthan. Even at times, the annual trips to Pokhara had seemed overwhelming. How would he cope in a city of over two and a half million people?

On the other hand, one less person in the household also meant extra food for everyone else in the family. It meant that there was a better chance that his baby brother would not go hungry. It meant that his father would not have to go ask others for help with food.

"Ram?"

He looked up at this father, realizing he had been silent for a while. He had been lost in his thoughts again.

"There may not be enough food for us all this winter. I want a better life for you, Ram, but the reality of the situation is that for the seven of us, it may just not stretch far enough this winter."

Ram nodded as he listened. This thought had already crossed his mind, but hearing from Baba made his stomach turn. His father was being practical as well as wanting the best for him. It was the man he had always known.

It was a lot to take in all at once, but he also had the feeling that the decision had already been made. This was not going to be discussed. And he understood how hard the coming winter was likely to be, based on how thin the past harvest had apparently been. What he also knew, in the back of his mind, was the horrible reputation that Kathmandu had for child labor.

There were laws to protect against possible abuses of such arrangements, but it was well-known that they were rarely, if ever, enforced. Ram realized that he was at a crossroads in his life, even if he was just twelve. He did not want to be an extra burden to his family. He wanted more out of his life. He had never been ashamed or embarrassed of his father, either. But he did want more.

A real education…it was what he had dreamed about for as long as he could remember. But for now, it seemed a done deal. His head was spinning….

3.

The Land Rover

While not completely unheard of, the sight of a car in Chandisthan was certainly not an everyday event. When one did pass through, all the kids in the village would run after the car to see where it would stop. Sometimes, they even received some candies from the tourists.

The day was a mix of sun and thick clouds as the olive Land Rover eased into the village. Kids tried to climb to the back of the Land Rover as it slowly navigated the narrow gravel roads of Chandisthan. There had been a growing crowd of locals gathering steadily near Ram's house, as the word of his new opportunity had spread quickly. Nothing remained a secret in this small, intimate village. Whether by women gossiping at the water fountain or men at the local tea shop, word spread fast. The vista back toward Kathmandu was open, too, and the trail of dust raised by the large vehicle had been impossible to miss, even as the wind picked up.

Ram and his parents stood unmoving in front of the house as the vehicle came to a stop near their fence. The fence was mostly only of name, made up of a couple of bamboo sticks and hemp ropes. The dust cloud from the road leading into the village got swept away by the gusts and was taken up and over the foothills of the mountains behind them. The gathered crowd stayed back and watched as a man and a woman emerged from the truck. The couple slowly moved towards the house, occasionally looking back at the crowd, still staring at them and the vehicle.

The man was short and lean with angular features, his face expressionless as he removed his sunglasses and looked out over the gathering. He had dark hair, cut close in an almost military-style manner. It seemed like he was starting to lose some hair in the front. He was dressed casually in simple black slacks and a white button-down shirt, but even in this unassuming dress, the man exuded an air of superiority.

Ram stared at the man's shirt, unable to believe how white it was. The shirt was flawless; there was not a smudge anywhere and it looked neatly ironed. The white shirts Ram saw in the village were closer to grey than white. The dust and dirt in the village would make it impossible to keep any white fabric white for too long. The man tucked his sunglasses away in a chest pocket of his leather coat and took a long and almost calculated survey of the village. It looked as if he just wanted to be done with his business and be on his way.

He was Nepalese, but to Ram, he exhibited none of the friendly and open and inviting characteristics that he had come to experience from his countrymen. It gave him a hollow feeling in the pit of his stomach. He smiled at the man broadly as he and the woman approached him and his parents. All he got in return was a neutral, almost cold stare back, as if he was looking *through* Ram, rather than at him. His face was expressionless. It was as if someone had glued all his face muscles in place so they would not move. It was either that or the man believed it was beyond him to smile at couple of village low-lives. Or, perhaps, it was just how the city people behaved. Regardless, this was all very new and strange to Ram.

He waited as the woman came around the vehicle to join him. The man seemed impatient and annoyed, even toward her. *Maybe the man does not really want to be here*, Ram thought. It took Ram by surprise when the man held out his hand to the woman and she took it as they walked together toward Ram's parents. Even this gesture seemed unnatural and emotionless to Ram.

Unlike the man, the woman was of medium build, almost bordering on chubby, but smiling. She seemed to be the complete opposite of him in every way imaginable. Rather than treat them as if they were just part of the scenery, the woman waved in a very friendly manner toward them as she came closer. Ram was sure she must be his wife.

"You must be Ram," the woman said as she gently patted him on his shoulder. That gut-twisting feeling of fear and uncertainty Ram had felt when he first saw the man began to lessen.

After a few moments, a third person emerged from the back seat of the Land Rover. This man was smaller and came out with clipboard in hand, the attached papers blowing wildly in the breeze. He also appeared to be Nepali and was dressed in a shirt and tie. *He must be the man's assistant*, Ram thought.

Ram's mother opened the door to the house and stood aside as the couple, the Nepali man with the clipboard, and then, finally, her husband entered. Ram's mother served tea to their guests and Ram's father asked him to wait outside. Following his father's order, Ram waited outside, wandering around alone as he pondered what his future might hold in store for him.

Some of the less curious in the village had gone back to their own places. A few remined behind, looking over the large vehicle that sat unattended along the road, touching it tentatively in wonder. The kids were still trying to climb on the vehicle and some were exploring inside through the window.

It was not that Ram did not want what this arrangement might have to offer; in fact, it was just the opposite. He knew his father was right— for him to get more out of his life, getting an education was the first step. He also knew that him being away meant more food for everyone else in the family. He was proud to be able to make this sacrifice to help his family.

He was not afraid of the hard work that being a household servant for these outsiders might require, either. He had worked very hard helping Baba and knew he could handle any kind of work. The thing that was making him reluctant and a bit anxious was that he would be leaving Chandisthan and everything he was familiar with behind. This is where he was born and grew up. Chandisthan was all he knew.

Most of all, he worried about saying goodbye to his parents. The excursions to Pokhara had always been exciting and something he looked forward to all year, but he had known it was just a trip. Eventually, they always returned home to their simple life in Chandisthan. He knew he would be back to his Ama's home-cooked meals. He knew he would be back to play with his little brothers and sisters.

This, however, felt like something more permanent. This felt *different*. He had been trying to ignore the thoughts that had begun filling his mind, but he could no longer ignore them. Ram realized that it might be a very long time before he would see Chandisthan and his family again. The scariest of all, however, was that he might never see them again. He had no idea what this situation might be all about, but in any case, it seemed as if it was out of his control now.

After about an hour or so, all five of the adults returned to the open area between the house and the Land Rover. Ram's mother was carrying a simple satchel, much like the type all the villagers used when they walked to another town or went exploring. It was a bit over-filled relative to what it might normally contain, but Ram recognized it immediately for what it was: a travelling bag. He could see that his mother had carefully packed his belonging in the tiny bag. He began to walk closer as his father and the Nepali man who had accompanied the couple bowed in the traditional manner, indicating the conclusion of a business transaction.

The local man turned and walked back to the vehicle, taking his seat in the rear, exactly where he had been when they all had arrived. Ram came to his parents and took the satchel from his mother as a tear ran down her face. The stalky city man simply turned on his heel after a quick handshake with Ram's father and got back behind the wheel of the Land Rover. The woman, whom Ram assumed was his wife, took Ram's mother's hands in hers and squeezed lightly. She glanced at Ram before making her own departure to the passenger's seat. Ram let the satchel fall at his feet as he faced his parents.

His father remained stoic, though Ram could see in his eyes that this moment was difficult for him to endure. He grasped Ram firmly by the shoulders, looked into his eyes, and offered a traditional Buddhist saying that had been passed down from generation to generation in his family:

"Aaphno herchar garnu babu. Khali bhando bata pani khanauna sakidaina."

Remember to take care of yourself. You cannot pour from an empty cup. Now more than ever, those words resonated with Ram. He struggled to keep his own tears at bay.

With that, Baba walked away and went inside, leaving just Ram and his mother alone in the wind and dying light of the day. Ram looked up at his mother as her tears fell more freely. She pulled him tight and Ram suddenly was as scared and sad as he had ever been in his life. He closed his eyes and tried to memorize every subtle touch and smell and sound of his mother that he could.

He had a feeling he was entering onto a new path for himself, and if he never saw her again, he wanted the moment to last him a lifetime. He wanted to be able to think back and draw on this embrace whenever he was feeling lost or depressed, so that he could use her strength to sustain him. The thought of never seeing his mother again scared Ram on a different level. Thoughts raced out of his mind as fast as they raced in. In the end, he knew the decision had already been made, and it was time for him to be a grown-up and fulfill his Baba's promise.

At long last, his mother released him and Ram took one long last look at her. He placed his hand on her face and wiped away her tears. Trying to be the grown-up he had to be now, he tried to comfort his mother.

"Ama, please don't cry. I want to remember your smile. I am going to work hard and study hard in the city. I will make you and Baba very proud. Do not worry about me. I am a grown boy now and I will take care of myself."

He could barely speak without crying, but he held his tears inside and continued.

"I will come visit during the festivals. I hope my brothers and sisters will still recognize me," he said with a slight smile on his face. "Ama, I know this is very hard right now. My love for you and Baba will never falter no matter how far I am from you two. I will think of you every day. After I study and become successful, I will take care of you and Baba so we do not have to worry about bad winters anymore. Please, take care of yourself."

Ram's father had come back outside and was standing by the wooden pillar at the front of their house. The look on his father's face was almost like the one he saw on the city man an hour earlier. There was no expression. It was as if all blood flow to Baba's face had stopped. The wrinkled face that usually bore a subtle smile showed nothing.

Ram moved over to Baba but could not bear looking him in the face. He knew Baba was trying to be strong and hold in his tears. He did not want to make this any more difficult on him by looking at his face. He longed to get one last look at Baba's gentle brown eyes, but he knew he would just have to rely on his memory.

He hugged his father's leg and touched his feet to get the blessing from his beloved father. Baba placed his hand on Ram's head as he got up to give him his blessing. There were no words exchanged and no tears shed. The heavy breathing and alternate sniffles said enough in that quiet moment.

He collected the satchel and moved toward the large vehicle. Ram had tried in vain to hold back his own tears, but now, he could no longer do so. Suddenly, he dropped the satchel, ran to his mother again, and cried into her arms as he had not done since he was very young. She dried his tears with the edge of her saree and gave him a kiss on his forehead. Ram retrieved the discarded bundle and walked resolutely to the waiting truck.

He opened the back door, tossed his belongings inside, and took a seat next to the local Nepali representative. Ram never looked back again. He was afraid he might break down again and he did not want this family to think of him as weak or childish.

He closed the door and the man spun the Land Rover in a tight arc, navigating them back toward Kathmandu. Ram just stared out the side window, watching the familiar sights of all he had known his entire life speed by. No one seemed to want to talk to him, so he closed his eyes as the vehicle bounced and jostled along the rough road. He fell into a quick, troubled sleep as the sun disappeared from sight.

4.

A New Light

Ram awoke as the ride suddenly changed from the rough rumble he was familiar with to the smoother, more improved roads near Kathmandu. What had also aroused him from his slumber was the noise. He had known that Kathmandu was likely to be buzzing with activity much busier than anything he had ever seen before, including Pokhara, but what he saw as he gazed out the window of the Land Rover was nothing he had really prepared himself for.

Even in the dark of the night, there were people and vehicles racing around. Cars, taxis, motor bikes, cycle-rickshaws, and bicycles sped by in all directions. *And the lights!* Ram had never experienced such a display of lights in his life! To a young boy from a small agricultural village, it was more than he could absorb. He supposed it was something he would get accustomed to, but presently, it just overloaded his senses. He closed his eyes to block out what he could as they crawled along with the flow of the traffic.

In another few minutes, they pulled over just out of the way of other vehicles to the loud and abrasive sound of other drivers expressing their frustration at the interruption. The man who had been sitting next to Ram got out and went to the driver's window. He removed a few of the papers from his ever-present clipboard and handed them to Mr. Kady. He bowed slightly as the man rolled his window back up and set off down the street, disappearing into the sea of people.

The Land Rover again entered the traffic to more horns. Ram wondered what the house he would be working and staying in would look like. They drove on for a few more minutes until they seemed to be leaving a lot of the congestion and noise of the city.

They began down a winding road that led into a greener and more secluded neighborhood. Ram could not see much due to the lack of lights in the dark, but at least the reduction in lights and racket was easier on his head. The car slowed and turned onto Maharajgung Road, then turned into a level spot in front of an enormous three-story structure.

After a lifetime in Chandisthan and his simple home in the village, Ram was stunned, his eyes wide as he looked upon the house. It was dimly lit from the outside, but Ram could see the multiple balconies that adorned each room on the upper floors and the lights that shone warmly from inside. *It was a palace!* At least to Ram it was. He thought these people must be some sort of near-royalty to live in such a place.

The driveway where they had parked was wide and covered with small stones, another smaller car sitting off to the side. The outside was a light orange or tan color, with teal-painted window frames. Ram was still sitting agog when he noticed that the woman was motioning to him to follow her inside.

He blushed, grabbed his satchel, and hurried along. The last thing he wanted to do was leave a poor impression with his benefactors. He hurried from the Land Rover and came alongside her as she walked into the house, using an entrance just beyond where the cars were left. She smiled at him, which made him feel welcome, but he noticed that her husband was nowhere to be seen.

She ushered him inside and what he saw here made the outside seem inconsequential. Ram was used to just simple pillows for seating and thin pads for sleeping. He looked around and saw the rooms filled with fancy furniture, more luxurious than anything he had ever seen.

The floors were made of wood and adorned with carpets woven in intricate, fascinating designs of oriental origin. Resting on the carpets were tables and matching chairs covered with delicate-looking fabric, and even electric lamps. All around on the walls were framed paintings and tapestry hangings. Ram had seen such things in the stores and cafés of Pokhara, but had never known anyone who might be able to afford such fineries. But as always, Ram was impressed, not jealous. Inspired, not envious.

As the woman walked through the house, Ram followed her so he could get acquainted with the layout of the house. She showed him a kitchen with all the ornate and mysterious accessories he had seen when he and his father had perused the market street of Pokhara.

And the bedrooms – *plural!* Ram had been so accustomed to the simple two-room house he had grown up in that to even imagine all these bedrooms was beyond his world. Each successive room was as elaborately furnished and decorated as the others. Ram felt a bit like an alien in this massive place.

He followed her back to the main room in which they had entered and sat when she gestured toward the chairs off to the side. Just as he sat down, a big smile appeared on Ram's face. There was, in the corner, the colorful box that took him to the dreamland. The Kadys had a television in their home. He was already imagining all the new things he would see in this box. All of the sudden, his tiredness disappeared and all he could think of was endless possibilities.

He was quickly pulled back to reality when he heard Mrs. Kady's voice.

"I am sorry we did not have time to talk before now, Ram, but it was a long drive and my husband was anxious to get home as soon as possible. He has to be up early tomorrow."

Ram just smiled and said nothing. It had been his experience with adults that this was often the best tactic when there was nothing of substance to add.

"Our name is Kady. My name is Sarita and my husband's is Nabin. We have two sons: Chandra, age thirteen, and Manu, age eleven. Please address us as Mr. or Mrs. Kady."

Ram thought this was an odd thing to emphasize, as he would have done this naturally. He supposed she just wanted a formal relationship.

"What I need help with here is to keep the house clean and assist with the meal preparation. The boys have assigned chores, too. Part of their duties is also food preparation, but I want you to help them out with that, as well."

Ram nodded and smiled.

"Both Mr. Kady and I work in town. There is just not enough time in the day anymore for me to attend to him and take care of the house and the boys as I would like. Do you understand?"

Ram nodded again. Looking around at the huge house, he had no idea how she had ever done this in the first place.

"You are quiet. How is your English? Do you even speak any English?"

"Oh, good, Ma'am. I learn from the trekkers that come to the Annapurnas near my village. They give me books. But I am hoping to learn more in school."

"Good. That is good. We speak Nepali and English, but we want both Chandra and Manu to speak proper English so they can be successful as adults. You can learn more from them."

Ram smiled and nodded to show his understanding.

"It is late. In the morning, you will meet the boys and receive a list of things we expect you to take care of. You can always come to me or the boys if you have questions. Do not bother Mr. Kady, though. He is very busy with his job."

Ram would not have done that anyway, based on his experience with Mr. Kady so far. Up until this point, he seemed like he was not too thrilled with having Ram around. *Maybe he just has a lot of other things on his mind*, Ram thought. *Like she said, he has a demanding job.* There were likely things here that he was unaware of. As always, Ram tried to look for the positive side of everything, no matter how it might appear.

"We have a place set up in the boys' room for you to sleep in."

Ram arose and followed her, his satchel over one shoulder. They padded down a long and dark hallway. She stopped and silently opened a door, stepping aside to allow him to enter the dimly lit room. He looked across the room and saw a simple pad on the floor, much like what he had at home. Ram was a bit surprised, based on how large the house was, that he was to sleep on the floor and in the same room as Chandra and Manu. He had not expected to have his own room, but this seemed peculiar.

Perhaps they wanted him to feel at ease, so they had tried to reproduce his environment from Chandisthan? Or maybe they were thinking he would get to know their sons better by having him share their room? It did not matter. He was sure he would be fine.

Besides, he was worn out from the day, both physically and emotionally, and he just wanted to sleep. He set his satchel to the side and lay on his back. As Ram lay across the pad on the floor, he tried to see this in the best way possible. Despite his fatigue, sleep suddenly would not come.

He missed his parents and the familiarity of Chandisthan. It would also be odd working for two boys his own age, but then again, maybe it would be like having his brothers around. It might be great fun.

Ram closed his eyes and tried to imagine this new life in that light, but all he could see was his mother's tears as he had said goodbye. Before he knew it, his face was damp, too.

5.

Badminton

Ram awoke early as the sun broke through the window of the bedroom and fell over his face. He was used to waking early for his meditations, anyway, and as the house still appeared fast asleep, he took the opportunity to do so.

He expressed his gratitude for this opportunity and asked Buddha to watch over his parents and protect them during the winter. He asked for guidance and direction in his new duties here at the Kady household and to let him learn all he could in school. As he was finishing, he looked up to see both Chandra and Manu staring at him.

"Who are you?" the one boy asked.

"Ram. I am here to help out with household chores."

"I am Chandra. This is my brother, Manu."

They nodded, but Ram could not help feeling like they were looking down on him—the look was very much like the one their father made when he came to Chandisthan to collect Ram. It was not as cold and dismissive, but was still apparent.

"What was that you were doing just now…sitting like that, with your eyes closed?"

"I was meditating and offering my gratitude."

The one boy rolled his eyes while the other snickered. Ram felt himself redden. He was not ashamed of his practice, but had just assumed that everyone did this. Apparently not. He wished he had held his tongue or made something up. *Maybe, though,* he thought, *this was just new to them. Maybe they are just curious. Or, maybe I just made my first mistake....*

The boys were about the same age as Ram, but they had a different aura and confidence to them. They wore clean clothes without any patches and had clear, fair skin. Ram had never worn clothes that were not hand-me-downs from someone they knew, patched again and again by his mother. His mom would quickly mend any tears. She would find pieces of fabric to attach to the shirts when they were too short for him. He wondered if he would get new clothes, too, now that he was in the city.

Just a second later, they all turned toward the window. The sound of the Land Rover crunching through the stones outside floated in as Mr. Kady drove off. The boys leapt from bed and ran out of the bedroom as the sound of their mother's voice called them to breakfast. Ram watched as they ran, unsure of what he should do. Was he to join them? He was not a family member. So, he sat and waited. Perhaps Mrs. Kady would call him, too. Ram waited, but he did not hear her call for him. Ram made up his little bed and walked out to greet her. Either he was to be included or he was to begin working. There was only one way to find out.

Ram wandered down the hallway and made his way to the sounds he could pick up around the corner. He took a quick peek into the living room to see if the TV was on. To his disappointment, it was still covered up. He walked into the kitchen, where Mrs. Kady and the boys were. He smiled weakly, but just stood still until someone said something. He looked like a regular kid whenever he smiled. His innocence covered his face when he smiled, showing those crooked yellow teeth.

"Ram, the boys are on vacation from school now for the winter break. I have to go to work, but I will have them leave you some food. Please clean up from breakfast. You will find an area just in the pantry that has a water tap and a place for you to wash dishes. Dry them when you are done. Then, sweep out all the rooms and take the trash out to the cans at the end of the driveway. That should keep you occupied until near dinner. The boys know about this. Watch them so you can learn how to prepare meals. Just assist them tonight."

Ram nodded, his smile fading from his face. He felt excitement, but also fear and uncertainty. This was a different woman than from the night before. She had seemed very friendly and nice then, but now, it was like that was just a dream. She was grim and stern in the face as she bent to clean up some broken pottery on the floor while she spoke to him. The boys seemed oblivious to his presence.

"Can you do that?"

"Yes, Mrs. Kady."

"Good. These will be your responsibilities for now. I would like you to use this winter school break to learn all about the house, then take on more of the food preparation. Once school starts again after the first of the year, you will be going to classes, so I want you to have a good handle on everything by then. Understand?"

"Yes, Ma'am."

There was something else in her speech and mannerisms that Ram could not quite figure out. Shouldn't she have just had him clean up the mess she was toiling over? It was almost like she was trying to hide the debris. And, he realized, she may have been crying; her eyes looked puffy and red. She looked both hurt and angry. Something had happened, he figured.

Maybe she was upset with her husband since he left so early? Maybe that was why she appeared so distant and cold to him today. On the other hand, he had to remind himself that he was not a family member. He was the hired help.

"Okay, boys, I am going to work. Make sure Ram has plenty to do and answer his questions if he has any. Are you still going to the center with your friends this morning?"

"Yes, mother," Manu replied.

She tossed a towel into the sink and grabbed a case, then waved goodbye and hurried out the door. Ram watched in silence as he heard the other car that was in the drive start up and small pebbles spray away in her wake. The boys dumped their plates in the sink and headed outside.

"Your breakfast is on the table, Little Buddha," Chandra called back over his shoulder. The brothers laughed together, clapping each other on the back, as they ran out. Ram was stung by the mocking comments.

Ram stood where he was, almost frozen in place. Was this how people in big cities acted? It was so foreign to the people he knew in Chandisthan. No one was ever this unkind and hurtful. What had he gotten himself into?

He closed his eyes and took deep breaths to rid his mind of the boys' taunting. He had hoped since they were of the same age, they would be like brothers, even if they were not real brothers. Perhaps he was just overreacting.

Ram shook off the experience and went to the table to find just a smattering of rice and dried-up looking lentils covered in some sort of thin, oily, yellowish-brown sauce. It was not what he was used to, but he would make the best of it. The taste of his mother's lentil curry stew came to him as he scooped some of the concoction into his mouth. *Eww!*

Not only was it cold and beginning to congeal, but it was bland— not at all what his mother would have made. He supposed if he tried hard enough, he could imagine the sauce to be a curry of some variety, but it was so weak! He did not know if this was how they ate all the time, or if it was another joke being made at his expense.

Ram choked down the plate of rice and lentils, as he was not sure when he might eat again. Despite the quality of the food, Ram made sure he was thankful for it as it was. He collected all the dirty dishes from the kitchen and carted everything over to the area in the pantry that Mrs. Kady had indicated was to be used for washing. There was just a hard brick of soap; it felt as hard as stone. The tap for rinsing was icy cold, only coming out in a slow trickle.

Ram sighed and set himself to the task. It took some effort, but once he got used to it all, he was able to clean everything with surprising results. He dried the dishes as she had instructed, then set about to the sweeping. It had not seemed like such a big deal when Mrs. Kady had mentioned it, but with all the rooms that were in the house, Ram found that the sweeping was an ordeal. He hummed old songs from his childhood in his head and dreamed of what it was going to be like to attend an actual school to make the task less daunting.

Once all the rooms were swept clean, Ram began to haul the trash from each to the large container he found at the end of the driveway. Just as he was finishing up, Chandra and Manu arrived home from the "center" that their mother had mentioned earlier. He was carrying the empty trash cans back to the house when they called to him.

"Ram! Want to play badminton with us?"

Ram stared, furrowing his brow. They held odd-looking devices in their hands, long wooden sticks with what looked like nets on the ends. In one hand, Chandra cupped this even weirder-looking cone-shaped object.

"Don't we have to make the evening meal?"

"Oh, come on. We've plenty of time before they get home for that. Want to play?"

Ram had no idea what badminton was, but it seemed like he was finally being accepted by the brothers and he did not want to cause any waves.

"I guess. What is it?"

Chandra smiled and waved him over.

"Watch us. You'll see."

Three of them walked over to small open area right next to the house. It was humid and chilly outside and the fog made for a low visibility. The boys were bundled up with winter clothes. With gloves, hat, sweater and boots, they were covered head to toe with warm clothes. Ram on the other hand was standing on the side shivering. Mrs. Kady had given him one of the boys' old sweaters but he had no gloves or hats. He could feel the damp cold in his toes with only slippers and no socks. He was however, excited to learn more about this new game and may be bond with the brothers little more.

They each stood on one side of a sagging wire stretched high between two trees that had a loose netting hanging from it. Chandra tossed the cone-shaped object into the air and batted it over the net to Manu, who pursued the object and batted it back before it hit the ground. This went on for several minutes until Manu batted the thing to a spot that Chandra could not reach and it fell to the ground.

"Get it?" Chandra asked as he went after the object.

"I think so," Ram replied, though it seemed to be a peculiar game. He and his friends had games back in Chandisthan, but nothing resembling this one. "Just hit it back and forth?"

"Yeah. Try and hit it to a spot where the other person is not, and if they cannot return it, you get a point. Grab the racket that is leaning against the tree and go join Manu. We can play you two against me, okay?"

Ram nodded and retrieved the racket. He joined Manu as Chandra prepared to begin the volley. The racket, Ram saw, did not have a net at the end as it appeared, but was stiff with crisscrossing fibers. He immediately saw how it worked. Chandra began the game and after a few awkward swings and misses, Ram began to get the hang of the game and found himself lost in the fun of it. The boys, likewise, laughed and yelled as they played with him. Ram was sure he had made two new friends, despite the rough start he had experienced with them.

The time went by, and Ram had forgotten all about the fact that he was there to work for the family. Just as it was his turn to serve, there was a screech of car brakes as Mrs. Kady slid to a stop and was marching across the yard toward them. They all froze and waited until she got closer.

"Ram! What do you think you are doing? You think we brought you here to play? You are here to work, not play!"

Ram felt the heat of embarrassment rise in his cheeks as she scolded him in front of Chandra and Manu. He dropped his eyes and set the racket and shuttlecock down at his feet.

"Have the dishes been cleaned?"

"Yes, Mrs. Kady."

"And all the rooms swept and the trash taken out, as I told you?"

"Yes, Ma'am."

"It had better be, for your sake!"

Ram felt tears welling up in his eyes, but he fought them back. He did not want to look like a baby to her.

"And you two! Is dinner making itself tonight?"

"No, mother," the boys replied in unison.

To Ram, it looked as if their response was so coordinated, that, perhaps, this was not the first time this had happened. They scurried off toward the house before their mother might get angrier, and Ram followed close behind so he could watch the process. Also, he did not want to have her attack him again. In all his years back home, Ram's mother had never raised her voice like that. He did not know if this was normal in this household or not, but he sure did not like it. He did not want to do anything that might make her any more displeased with him.

He did not look back, but hurried after Chandra and Manu as they bustled into the kitchen. They began gathering ingredients for dinner, as well as the pots and pans that were needed to fix the meal. Ram hung off Chandra's shoulder and watched carefully, only moving when he was asked to do a simple chore, such as washing a vegetable or slicing up one of the ingredients. Manu peeked out the window and saw that his mother was still fuming in the yard. Ram could not help but notice the knowing glances between the brothers as they worked on the food preparation.

He was not sure, but he thought he had noticed a sly wink from Chandra toward Manu as they both grinned and continued their chore. Ram was sure that, by joining in on the badminton game, he had made some progress toward a connection with them. But now, it seemed as if it had all been a setup to put him in a bad light with their mother.

Ram had let his natural openness and trust in people, and perhaps even naiveté, get him in hot water again. This type of devious and underhanded behavior was not an experience that Ram was accustomed to. He would not let it happen again, if possible. He was learning – even if it was the hard way.

6.

Empty Vessel

Ram watched the boys intently as they got the meal together and began the cooking. It was a simple procedure and Ram was sure he could do this right away. Maybe taking on this chore might make Mrs. Kady more pleased with him and make her forget about this afternoon.

As the light of day faded, Ram heard the Land Rover pull up and the even, heavy steps of Mr. Kady approaching the house. The door opened and closed with a louder slam than Ram thought was necessary. The boys started picking up items scrambled near them to make sure everything was in order. There was a sudden change in their expression. It seemed that their face showed fear more than excitement with their father getting home. He stood still and confused as Mr. Kady tossed his coat aside and glared at Ram.

"Boy! Come here!"

Ram cowered at the sound of his bellow, but he approached timidly, figuring that avoiding it or not responding might make matters worse. The man's face was red with anger and Ram was afraid he might strike him. He had no idea what he must have done to have incurred such anger, but he saw that both Chandra and Manu turned away, their smirking expressions now pale and frightened. They apparently knew well of their father's temper. He was shaking as he slowly walked towards Mr. Kady. He could not dare look at Mr. Kady or say anything until he was spoken to.

When Ram got within an arm's reach of him, Mr. Kady reached out and grasped a handful of Ram's shirt collar and began marching him back out of the house and toward the driveway. Mrs. Kady shrank back and pressed herself into the doorframe, just watching the spectacle as the two of them shot past her.

Ram struggled to keep his feet moving; Mr. Kady was nearly lifting him off the ground as he rushed him along. They moved through the driveway and just outside the entrance to the property, where Ram fell in a heap as the man released his grip without warning.

Ram stood and brushed dirt from his pants. He looked up to a still glowering Mr. Kady as he simply pointed toward the trash bin that was situated nearby. Ram followed the pointed finger of the man to see that the bin was on its side, the contents scattered across the road. He had no idea how this had happened, as it had all been contained in the upright can when he had emptied all the trash from the house earlier in the day.

"Is this what we hired you for, boy? May be it is fine in your dirty village to have trash scattered all over." Mr. Kady's voice was now trembling as he continued, his voice raised so loud that the whole neighborhood could hear him. " This is the city, and I am a well respected person here. What will people think if they come to visit me and see this mess at the entrance of the house? Is this how your parents raised you?"

The sound of his voice was now even more menacing than before. Ram bowed his head in shame as he shook it back and forth slowly. The last sentence had hurt the most. Ram thought there was no need to blame his parents for his mistakes. He was near tears, but he fought them back.

"Well? Pick it up. *Now!*"

Ram scrambled across the road, gathering all the debris and depositing it all again in the container after having set it upright. As he worked frantically under the heated stare of Mr. Kady, Ram was baffled as to what had happened.

Then, he thought of Chandra and Manu and how they had tricked him into the game to get him in trouble with their mother. In his heart, he sincerely hoped he was wrong, but he began to wonder if this was another of the boys' pranks to make him look bad. He finished and looked up timidly at Mr. Kady.

"I am sorry, sir. I was sure I had secured the can. It will not happen again."

Ram saw no point in trying to explain what was most likely the reason for the mess. He had no proof. He was just the house boy; the man was not likely to believe him over his sons.

"It had better not! We are giving you a fine place to live, feeding you, and soon, we will be paying for your school, as well! You had better start doing your job, or we can find someone else who can and you will find yourself on the street! Do I make myself clear?"

"Yes, Mr. Kady. I am very sorry."

Ram stayed unmoving, still fearing that he might suffer a blow from the man. He trembled slightly as he prepared for it. After a few seconds, he looked up to see that he was alone. Mr. Kady was stomping back to the house. He was not sure what to do at this point, but gradually, he collected himself and returned to the kitchen. He just wanted to finish helping with dinner and then disappear to his sleeping pad in the boys' room.

However, once he came back, Ram found that there was more displeasure coming his way. Mr. Kady was nowhere to be seen, but he walked into the kitchen to find Mrs. Kady holding a single plate up so he could see the surface. She looked as upset as her husband had been earlier. Ram came to a sudden standstill and just looked at her.

"Ram? Is this one of the plates that you cleaned this morning?"

To Ram, this was a nonsensical question. The family had only one set of dishes, and surely, she must have known that it was. It puzzled him, but he replied anyway.

"Yes, Mrs. Kady."

"Why, then, is it not clean?"

Ram looked hard at the plate, but as hard as he stared, he could not see what she was talking about. He knew enough now not to contradict her. He had been brought up to respect adults no matter what. Ram bowed his head and, once again, offered his apologies.

"I am sorry, Mrs. Kady. I will be more thorough in the future."

"I hope so. What my husband just said to you? I hope you fully understood him, because I would not want to have to repeat his warning."

"Yes, Ma'am. I understand. I will do a better job. I promise."

She laid the dish on the table with a solid thunk. With that, spun on her heels and strode from the kitchen, joining her husband at the dining table in the adjoining room. Ram closed his eyes and pushed away all the anger and abuse he had just endured. He knew he was beholden to this family for what they were providing him with. He did not want to bring disgrace to his own mother and father by failing at this opportunity.

If he did not get better at the Kadys' requests, he was not sure what he would do or where he would go. They had made it clear that if he did not improve, he might find himself on the street – not back in Chandisthan, but on the streets of Kathmandu. The mere thought of that petrified Ram.

He moved back to rejoin Chandra and Manu as they put the finishing touches on dinner. He followed their instructions as he helped them bring the meal to the table, where their parents were seated. As Ram helped the boys set the dishes on the table, Chandra and Manu took empty seats there with their parents. Both the adults seemed to have calmed down following their tirades against Ram, and were talking peacefully with each other about their day. Ram stood obediently by, afraid to move, just waiting for his orders.

"That is all, boy!" Mr. Kady snapped as he spread a napkin in his lap. "When we are done, we will call for you to clear the table. Once you have done that and thoroughly washed the dishes, then you may eat. I understand that your ability to clean dishes is as bad as your ability to take out trash? This will not be tolerated. Leave us!"

Ram nodded in humility and backed out of the dining area. He returned to the kitchen to begin cleaning up the pots and pans. This time, though, he could not stop the tears as he collected all the dirty cookware and made his way to the pantry to begin scouring them. He did them several times, just to make sure they were really clean.

He was fighting his emotions unsuccessfully and was glad he was well-removed from the family so that they could not see him. His tears finally stopped as he scrubbed and scrubbed, thinking back to his father's parting words of advice.

Babu, aaphono herchaha garnu. Khali bhando bata pani khanauna mildaina.

Indeed, Ram thought. *If I am an empty vessel, then I am of no use to anyone. Not to myself, not to the Kadys, not to the aspirations my parents have for me.*

Ram straightened his back, wiped his eyes, and set about making sure he did not fall short this time. He inspected the cookware closely and was sure it was all spotless, then dried them and returned them to the cabinets in the kitchen. Just as he was finishing up, he heard Mrs. Kady call for him to collect the dishes from the table. Ram hurried to obey.

He did not make eye contact with anyone as he worked. He returned to the pantry to repeat the process, taking extra care to make sure they were all very clean. He was exhausted as he finished up, his hands raw and sore from the texture of the soap block and the cold water from the tap.

When he got to the kitchen, he found a small plate on the table that he assumed was his dinner. No one was around and all the lights in the house were out, except for a dim lamp on the table next to his dinner.

Ram sat at the table and looked at the plate. It was not at all representative of what he had served the family. There had been bowls of steaming vegetables, an enticing platter of lamb smothered in a rich, thick, golden-brown sauce, and rice. Ram's plate, however, had just a layer of rice with a few pieces of the lamb scattered about. The meat was not the juicy cuts he had seen, but remnants clinging to the bones that looked as if they had been picked over before being discarded. The vegetables were sad and wilted, as well, likely the pieces that were not wanted.

It was a step up from his morning meal, but not by much. Ram and his family had never eaten meat very often, anyway, so he just shrugged it off. The sauce was weak and a bit bland for Ram's tastes, nothing even remotely like what his mother made regularly.

He pushed the bones and attached meat aside and dug into the rice and vegetables. Luckily, there was lots of rice left over, and he refilled his plate from the bowl he had not yet discarded and cleaned up.

Like always, Ram took the time to express his gratitude for the food and for the opportunity he had been offered with the Kadys. He asked for guidance, strength, and assistance in pleasing this demanding family so that he could remain in their employ and get his education. After cleaning his own dishes, Ram walked quietly down the hall to his sleeping pad, making sure not to cause any noise that might awaken anyone or draw any more attention to himself.

The boys appeared to be asleep when he laid down. Ram settled into his bed on the floor with a subdued sigh of fatigue. He fell asleep right away and was grateful for this, as he was sure tomorrow was likely to be another long day. He hoped his efforts would be more acceptable. It was unlikely the Kadys would tolerate more of what they saw as shortcomings on his part.

Ram did sleep, but his dreams were filled with torment, angst, and abuse from all sides. Every time he looked into the faces of those filling his nightmares, it was the Kadys – both the parents *and* the sons.

7.

Mount Everest

The days rolled by for Ram. There had not been another major blow-up with the Kadys. He was getting more and more comfortable with his role in the family as time went on, but he was always on guard for another sudden or inexplicable outburst.

The one thing that Ram had come to observe was that Mr. Kady had a volatile and seemingly uncontrollable temper. He had seen Mrs. Kady and both boys become the targets of it. It was so unlike any of the adults he had grown up around in Chandisthan. Maybe it was the pressures of his job or the big city? Maybe it was just who he was.

Mr. Kady had a difficult personality to decipher. It seemed strange how quick his mood changed. Mr. Kady was a gentle, soft-spoken man most times. He seemed to genuinely care for and love his family. He was like a parent to Ram most times, too.

The problem was that there was no way of telling when his mood was going to change. He could be in a somber mood, watching television or talking on the phone with his colleagues. Mr. Kady loved talking on the phone. He would answer the phone no matter what he was doing. It did not matter whether they were having dinner or if he was helping the boys with their homework, if the phone rang, he would spring up from his chair to pick it up before it rang three times. He could be happily chatting with his colleagues on the telephone, hang up and walk over to the boys or Ram and all of the sudden, burst out in the river of rage that no one could see coming.

Anytime Mr. Kady had to repeat an order more than twice, he was sure to blow up. His face would turn red and the blood vessel in his left temple would pop up to a size of a straw. It almost seemed like another person took over Mr. Kady's body. It was not uncommon for him to throw whatever was near him amid his blow up. Then, within half an hour, he would be back to normal. It was like nothing ever happened, and he would be his usual soft-spoken and compassionate self.

It was difficult to tell if he completely forgot what happened or if he was just trying to mask it and move on. In some instances, he seemed to feel guilty as he spoke to his family. He would try to change the conversation topics to something exciting. He never came out and apologized to anyone, but remorse and guilt could be seen in his eyes.

Fortunately, though, Ram seemed to have been pleasing the man as of late. Other than some minor corrections to what he was doing for them, all had been relatively calm since that initial attack. He could not remember the last time a plate had come flying at him. This was good progress.

Mrs. Kady seemed to be a regular target of his, though, and Ram understood now what had happened during his first morning with them. He had witnessed Mr. Kady flying into rages over virtually nothing, and inanimate objects in the house would be destroyed as a result. That was likely what happened then.

He thought back to Mrs. Kady cleaning up the mess of broken pottery that morning. She looked visibly upset and like she had been crying. And there was this look about her when her husband was home that reminded him of a frightened animal. She was jumpy and nervous around him. It all fit together. The environment around the house was completely different when Mr. Kady was gone for a long trip. Everyone seemed to be at ease and relaxed. Mrs. Kady and the boys smiled and laughed more. This usually carried over to Ram as well.

The one remaining issue for Ram was that she constantly was nagging at him to do more and more. Also, no matter how thorough he was with the kitchen clean-up, it seemed she was never satisfied with the cleanliness of the dishes and cookware.

It was really a minor issue for Ram now, and he thought it might have more to do with her needing an outlet for her pent-up fear of her husband's tirades. Ram just continued to apologize and re-do whatever it was that she was not happy with. It had become more of a ritual to Ram than anything serious. She constantly reminded him of how tough life had been for her when she was growing up and going to school. It was like she needed to vent her frustration and he was handy. He just took it in stride and carried on. School would be starting soon, and it would all be worth it just for that.

On one day, though, Ram had to agree with Mrs. Kady about the dishes. She came to him with a visibly soiled plate and he was shocked to see what she had discovered. It was definitely *not* clean, and Ram knew for sure that he would have not put away anything in that condition. He re-scoured the ones that were still dirty, but could not for the life of him figure this out. It just made no sense.

One evening, after dinner, Ram was busy in the pantry finishing up one last skillet that had been used that night for a stir-fry meal. He heard some quiet steps outside the room, back in the kitchen, and he snuck a peek around the corner. In the dim light of the room, he spied Chandra lifting the top half of a stack of clean dishes and setting them aside so that there were two identical stacks of plates.

Ram stared and held his breath so as not to be discovered and watched as the boy was putting food scraps back on some of the clean plates. He then systematically mashed the inserted food bits between the plates and reorganized them into their original stack.

From all outward appearances, the plates still looked clean, the soiled ones being hidden in the pile. After all this time, Ram was hoping that the boys would be more accepting of him, but this made it clear that they were not. Manu seemed friendlier lately, but there was definitely a vindictive streak in Chandra. Perhaps, he thought, it was again some fallout from his father's behavior. Ram had no idea why he would lash out at him in this regard, but otherwise, it was just mean and disrespectful. Maybe, the boys were trying to keep their father's focus on Ram to avoid drawing any attention to them.

Ram waited until Chandra tiptoed away, thinking he had gotten away with his prank. Now, Ram had an idea why the dishes had become such a topic of displeasure with Mrs. Kady. He separated the stack and once more made sure all had been properly cleaned before returning all of them to the cabinets. It would be an interesting morning tomorrow when Chandra found all the dishes spotless. This must have become a real source of entertainment for him.

The next morning, Ram arrived early in the kitchen, as had become his pattern. He was now doing most of the meal preparation and he needed the extra time in the morning to have a separate breakfast set up before Mr. Kady appeared. He usually left for work well before the others were up and Ram was trying hard to accommodate all the different schedules of all the family.

Mr. Kady entered the dining room and Ram brought him his normal fare. He had graduated from "boy" to Ram with him now, and Ram saw that as real progress.

Mr. Kady was quiet, which was often a sign of a volcano about to blow. But as he sat and Ram brought him his food, he smiled and thanked Ram. It was so unexpected that Ram was stunned for just a few seconds before replying. He quickly hurried back to the kitchen. Ram smiled to himself as he busied with the next phase of the meal for the others, feeling like maybe a corner had been turned with his major tormentor.

Mrs. Kady was next to appear, coming to the kitchen first to inspect the dishes from the previous night's meal. This was not unusual. It had become a ritual, like a military inspection. Ram stood to the side as she looked over all the dishes and cookware with a close eye.

"Wonderful, Ram! Thank you for making the extra effort. This is what I want!"

Ram just returned her smile and nodded as she went to join her husband at the dining room table. He set out the plates and glasses for breakfast, bringing Mrs. Kady her favorite Orange Pekoe tea. Then, he cleared away the used dishes at Mr. Kady's place. Mr. Kady offered a quick kiss to his wife, then strode through the kitchen and into the Land Rover to head off to work.

"You can bring in the food, Ram."

Ram nodded and went to fetch what he had been keeping warm.

"Chandra! Manu! Breakfast is being served, boys!"

Ram held back in the kitchen until the boys were seated with their mother before entering with his tray bearing the morning meal. He looked slyly over at Chandra, who did not disappoint him. The boy could not hide his confusion and puzzlement at the sparkling clean plate before him. Ram was not sure, but he guessed that the lack of the normal criticism of his efforts from his mother was baffling him. He served them all and shot a knowing look Chandra's way as he tucked the tray under his arm.

"Would there be anything else, Mrs. Kady?"

"No, Ram. This looks wonderful. Thank you."

Ram shot Chandra one more glance before departing to begin the clean-up. He had a spring in his step this time, though, as he clearly saw the sheepish and guilty look on the boy's face. Chandra had been found out and Ram did not need to even say anything.

Nothing more was ever said between Ram and Chandra about the issue. Ram had found a way to put a stop to the nonsense without trying to bring this to the attention of his parents, even if they might have believed him. He felt like he had climbed Mount Everest!

It was not like he and Chandra were now great friends, but there were no more pranks being performed at his expense. A kind of peaceful co-existence had emerged between the three of them. Now, all that Ram had to watch out for was the unpredictable Mr. Kady.

He still had moments of anger, but Ram just kept his head down and went about his tasks as requested. He figured as long as he did what was asked of him, he was safe from the occasional eruptions. These days, Mr. Kady tended to take out his annoyance or irritations on his wife and his sons, rather than Ram.

He felt bad for them, but there was not much he could do to help other than provide some relief with his role as their house boy.

8.

Birthday Cake

The winter break from school was ending soon, and Ram was almost vibrating with excitement as he anticipated his first classes. He dreamed what schools in the city might be like. His school in the village was not exactly close to his house. Just the idea of not having to walk two hours to get to his school excited him.

He vaguely remembered those early childhood days of endless walking. He was scared to cross the river in the beginning but had become excellent at rowing the small boat across the river. The school building itself was an old mud hut with a tin roof. The roof heated up so much in the summer that the room seemed like a sauna.

Then, when the monsoon started, that patchwork of a roof did a terrible job protecting them from the rain. He could not even remember the number of days when he ran to school only to go home half an hour later because the rain was too strong. Even if the roof shielded all the rain, the loud noise from the rain falling on the tin roof made it impossible to teach. Things would definitely be different in the big city.

He spent what little free time he had re-reading the well-worn copy of *The Old Man and the Sea* that he had brought with him from home. It did not have a wide range of English for him to practice on, but it was better than nothing. Ram wanted to be as prepared as possible when school began.

There was no shortage of books at the Kadys' house. It seemed like every room had a large bookcase filled with all sorts of books. Mr. Kady was proud of all the books he had. Almost anytime there was a new guest at home, Mr. Kady would unlock one of his bookcases and grab a book out to tell stories to his guests. All these stories were not stories from the books, but mostly stories about where he got the book or how smart he was to understand the topics in them.

Ram never understood why the bookcases were always locked. There were a couple of times when he was given the key, with strict instruction on which book to bring and to not touch anything else in there. However, it never stopped Ram from standing in front of the bookcases and staring at colorful covers, imagining what stories each of them might hold.

He was happy that no one could take away his beloved book that the nice American tourist, Mr. Garrison, had given him years ago. His vivid imagination made his old book new every time he went through it.

Before that, however, there was the impending celebration of Manu's twelfth birthday. He was aware of the passing of each year, but the idea of recognizing and celebrating a new year in one's life was foreign to Ram.

There was much excitement and activity around the Kady residence in preparation for the event, and Ram was fascinated by it all. He had been busy in the kitchen, preparing food for the celebration in addition to his normal responsibilities. There was supposed to be some sort of sweet delicacy to accompany the rest of the food that Ram was setting up. Ram wondered what it might be.

On the day of the event, Ram stood in awe and wonder as a delivery man dropped off this towering creation, the top of which was decorated with designs of a fancy flourish, surrounding the words "Happy Birthday Manu". It was like nothing Ram had ever seen before.

He was informed that this was a birthday cake. He was well acquainted with cakes in general, but he had never heard of anything called a birthday cake. It looked wonderfully magical. Ram stared at it as he waited for the last of the main dishes to be served at this gathering.

Lots of Manu's friends from school and the neighborhood had begun to arrive and they were busy playing various games outside while Ram toiled away. Ram carted all the dishes that he had made for the party out to long tables covered with colorful paper and set them in rows, along with plates and dishes for the guests. He then retreated to the kitchen to begin cleaning up. He listened to the laughter and shouts of the people outside as they celebrated Manu's day.

Ram was still curious about the whole thing. From what he heard, it reminded him very much of the celebrations held in Chandisthan to mark the end of a successful harvest season or the end of winter and the advent of the new spring. But this extravagant gala for a young boy just because he was another year older? He just did not get it.

Ram watched from a hidden vantage point in the kitchen once his chores were completed. Even though it was a new experience for him, he was enthralled as he watched. It looked like such fun and he felt a bit sad that he had never had such a celebration in his honor. He thought if he ever had kids, he would throw birthday party like this for them.

After a few minutes, the crowd gathered around the cake and began to sing a song. The song had a nice melody to it. Ram's English, though better than most of his neighbors' from Chandisthan, was still quite crude compared to the residents of Kathmandu. By sheer repetition, Ram picked up most of the words by the time it ended and the crowd broke into an enthusiastic round of applause for Manu. He looked away as Mrs. Kady began slicing off sections of the cake and passing them around to all the guests. Ram sat quietly in the dark of the kitchen and wondered what it must feel like to be the center of so much attention and adulation.

He had never felt neglected at all as he had grown up, but to have the day he was born raised to such heights? He felt simultaneously sad and intrigued. Then, the thought came to him.

When is my birthday?

Ram had never even wondered about such a thing before. It was just not an event that had been observed in Chandisthan. The village was successful or struggled based on the efforts of the collective population, not the individual. They all helped each other out. No one was ever singled out for anything. Ama made rice pudding for him on a day around festival time in honor of his birthday but no one knew when his actual birthday was. It usually happened on a day when there was enough milk and supplies to make the dish. It was, to Ram, not better or worse, but just different. Previously, he had not given it any thought, but now....

Ram felt himself lost in a whirlwind of conflicting emotions. He nearly missed his name being called in an almost whispery voice that was coming from the back entry to the pantry. It was Manu. He was calling to Ram, but it was obvious that he was trying to keep his visit secret. Ram had no idea what he might want. If there was something else needed at the party, he was sure he would have been summoned in a more direct manner by Mr. or Mrs. Kady.

He looked over after shaking away the cobwebs of his daydream and saw Manu calling to him, gesturing emphatically for him to come closer. With Manu, Ram had no worries. Of the two brothers, Manu had always been the kinder and gentler. If this had been Chandra, Ram might have been suspicious. But it was Manu, so he just got up and went.

As he reached the opening where the pantry door was ajar, Ram saw that Manu was handing him a small slab of the cake. He hesitated, afraid that he might get in trouble. Manu was making it apparent that he needed to take the plate quickly before he was discovered.

"For you, my friend, on my birthday. You work so hard for us and we have not always been nice to you. I wanted you to have some cake and celebrate , but I must not stay away long. Father and Mother might not approve."

Ram was speechless. He held the plate in his hands and looked out as Manu scrambled back to the gathering before he might be missed. Then, he looked down at the delicious-looking confection before him. It was a touching gift – not just that Manu had brought him cake, but that he had called him "my friend". It was the first real gesture that anyone here had made toward him since he had arrived indicating any sense of caring or consideration.

Tears from his cheek dripped onto the corner of the plate. He wanted to hug Manu and thank him. It seemed like he had finally won over the Kady boys. He was starting to feel like a part of the brotherhood. He was feeling loved and appreciated.

Ram smiled, wiped his face, and dug into the cake, realizing that he might be called for any minute to begin collecting all the dirty dishes from the party. He took a huge bite of the cake and could not believe how wonderful it was. The cake itself was soft and moist, tasting of vanilla and sugar. It was slathered with icing that made the cake itself seem bland. The two textures together made Ram smile wide. Ram had never tasted anything similar.

He rushed the rest of the piece into his mouth, relishing each morsel, knowing he had never tasted such a treat. He set the plate aside and licked the last bit of icing from his fingers just as he heard Mr. Kady shout for him to come.

Ram shot to his feet, suddenly remembering where he was and why he was there. He could not, though, seem to wipe the enormous smile from his face as he fell back into his role as a servant to the Kadys. He ran around and attended to his chores in the yard as Manu said goodbye to all his guests, a huge grin on his face all the while.

Nabin looked at Sarita with a furrowed brow and she just shrugged.

"Maybe he is just happy about being around all this excitement? He has probably never seen such an event before."

Nabin nodded in agreement and went back to the yard to see off the last of the crowd. The small but significant gesture from Manu lifted Ram up and helped make the extra work after the party less of an ordeal. He could still taste the sweet sugar from the icing in his mouth and remember the indescribable texture and flavors from the cake as he worked.

On one of his last passes in and out of the kitchen, Ram caught Manu walking by to go to bed. He waved and mouthed, "thank you."

He did not want him to get in any trouble with his parents for his generosity and big-heartedness. Manu waved back and just smiled.

The rush of sugar from the cake soon left Ram as he worked late into the night, scouring all the many extra dishes from the celebration. Just as his eyes were almost too heavy to hold open any longer, he saw that the last bowl had been done, and he plodded wearily toward his pad in the boys' room. He collapsed with a fatigue he had not known before and fell into a deep and peaceful slumber.

*****

In the middle of the night, Chandra and Manu were awakened by low but audible sounds coming from Ram as he slept. Chandra just laughed and rolled back over, facing away from the mumbling Ram.

Manu, however, pushed his covers aside and walked closer so he could hear what Ram was saying in his sleep. Ram's words were coming in fits and spurts, and seemed to be a bizarre mix of English and Nepali. Manu sat close by and listened. Ram seemed to be repeating a phrase over and over.

But the longer he listened, he realized it was not just spoken words, but that they had a rough, lyrical lilt to them. He knew that Ram spoke a bit of English, but that it was still not extensive.

Manu was puzzled for a long time, then finally just gave up and went back to his bed. He had no more than closed his eyes when it dawned on him what Ram was trying to say. He had been trying to sing along from what he must have heard at the party.

He was trying to say, "Happy Birthday to Ram."

The poignancy of the moment touched Manu, despite his young age. For the first time since Ram had arrived, Manu understood all that Ram and his family had sacrificed to send him here to work.

He had never thought of himself and Chandra as entitled with all they had. But now, it was beginning to sink in for him that others might not be as fortunate. Manu recalled a speech that their father had given them when they first moved to the city years ago.

"Sons, you are starting a new school today. There will be a lot of students who have more than us and you might wonder why we do not have the same things as them. It is important to keep in mind that there are also a lot of people who have less than you. Never show off what you have or be jealous of what others have!"

After a brief pause, he had added, "It is completely fine to strive to have better life for yourself, but remember to thankful for all that you have, too."

Manu had never really understood what their father was trying to say – until today. All of the sudden, Manu had a newfound compassion and appreciation for Ram.

9.

Penance

Relations between the brothers and Ram began to warm up quite a bit as the new school session approached. Ram was not sure if Manu had been the influence or not, but the relationship he now had with them was vastly different then it had been just a month earlier.

Maybe, Ram thought, it was because Chandra's latest prank on Ram had gotten blown up without any parental intervention. Or, maybe his warmer connection with Manu had been an influence. Whatever the case, Ram was feeling more at ease now, which was good since he was already on edge with his classes about to begin.

He knew that, even though he was about the same age as both Chandra and Manu, he was likely to be entered into a lower level of instruction. His tentative grasp of English was a big part of that.

Ram had always thought that his English was good, but the more time he spent in Kathmandu and was around the people there, the more he came to understand that what he had picked up from his lone book and from the tourists in Khudi Bazaar was very rudimentary. This did not deter him, though. He was sure that with the proper motivation and dedication, he could excel.

Just prior to his first day of school, Ram found out that Mr. Kady would be away from the house for an extended trip. All Ram knew was that it was related to his job, but that he would be travelling to both New Delhi and Bombay. Ram knew only of the cities from maps, but the thought of being able to travel freely see other foreign lands seemed like a wonderful adventure.

He wondered if Mr. Kady was going to visit all those colorful places he saw in the TV. If Mr. Kady was going to be in the places shown in TV, did that mean Mr. Kady might be on TV, too? His wild imagination quickly took over again.

He met with both Mr. and Mrs. Kady a few days before his departure so that they could make sure that Ram understood what the new routine would be while he was away. It was to be a bit less demanding, Ram figured, as it was one less person to make special arrangements for at meal times. And on top of that, he imagined that it would be a bit less stressful just to have Mr. Kady's sudden fits of anger removed for a while. There also seemed to be an aura of relief from Mrs. Kady, who had become the primary recipient of his temper lately.

Ram retreated to his small space in the bedroom to mentally and emotionally prepare himself for the beginning of school. The rest of the family went to bid farewell to Mr. Kady as he set off for India.

As Ram had expected, the daily routine for the family was much easier to adhere to with just the boys and Mrs. Kady around. There did seem to be a lighter air at the house, as well. Ram often saw Mrs. Kady smiling more and laughing and joking with Chandra and Manu—something that he could not recall having seen since he arrived.

Chandra and Manu helped Ram get settled that first day of classes and promised to wait for him after school so that they could walk back home together. It was another unexpected gift, and Ram made a mental note to make sure he included this in his meditations of gratitude that night.

School was more of a challenge then Ram had anticipated. Besides being placed in classes with much younger children while he worked to get his English up to par, there was the inevitable teasing from the children that he had to endure. Ram shrugged it off as best he could; he could not afford distractions as he tried to balance his lessons with all his ongoing responsibilities for the Kadys.

One day, though, the jeers and teasing just stopped. Ram did not know why, but was just grateful it had. That evening, after he had finished his chores and was going over his studies in the bedroom, Manu filled him in. Chandra was out and Manu knew his brother might like to have it kept a secret. He sat with Ram and told him why, only with the promise that he never tell Chandra.

"Do you remember when we were walking home last week and you mentioned to us that the kids were poking fun at you?"

"Yeah. It was just conversation, though. It was no big deal."

"Well, that is not how Chandra saw it. He has come to understand how hard this is for you. You know, leaving your family behind to work for us and go to school. He feels bad for all the things he did to make it harder for you when you arrived."

Ram just sat quietly and took all this in.

"Like myself, he has come to value you, both as our helper here in the house and now, as a friend. He had a...shall we say...talk...with the children in your class that were pestering you. He made sure they understood that this was to stop."

"Really?"

Manu nodded. "He is looking out for you, Ram. Me, too."

"Shouldn't I thank him, though?"

"No! Absolutely not. It is important to Chandra that you not know of this. That is why this must be kept just between you and me. I thought you would like to know, but he was adamant that you not discover it."

"Okay. But why?"

"I think it is part of the penance Chandra wants to pay for his behavior earlier. I am not sure, really, but he made it clear that this was to remain private. Promise me, okay?"

"I promise."

Ram's lessons did not get any easier, but having had the taunting of his classmates removed helped. Each week his English got a little bit better. Both Chandra and Manu spent time drilling him when they could to push him along. They all realized that for Ram to really understand the other parts of his classes, he would have to make big leaps in his English comprehension. The other competing factor was that he often could not spend as much time studying and doing assigned material as he would like, since his household chores were still very demanding.

The boys knew they could not intervene with his work in the house, as this was their parents' domain. However, when Ram sometimes could not finish his assignments or was having a difficult time understanding them, they would step in to help him.

Again, it was usually Chandra who took the lead in this assistance, as he hated to see Ram struggle so much. He knew he was working as hard as he could, so he and Manu were there to support him. On days when Ram's household chores had obviously taken too much out of him to allow him enough time to finish critical homework, the brothers would make sure any missing work was completed for him.

*****

About a month after he left for India, Mr. Kady returned home, all smiles and in a mood that Ram had never seen before. Ram went to the Land Rover to help Mr. Kady bring his things into the house, and the man thanked him.

The trip had apparently been a huge success and he had accomplished everything that his Kathmandu office had expected of him. Ram saw Mrs. Kady and the boys relish in his return, none of the signs of his usual short fuse or frustration anywhere to be seen.

Ram took his suitcases and began the laundry from them, as had been requested. The family sat in the living area and told stories of all that had happened in his absence. Ram hoped that this was a new trend, and not just a temporary thing that would vanish after time. It was a different man than he had seen so far. Maybe the trip had been so successful that Mr. Kady would be less stressed now at home.

Ram had taken all of his bags except for one large woven bag, which Mr. Kady had hung onto as he moved to the living area to reconnect with his family. Between trips in and out of the kitchen and laundry area, Ram peeked into the warmly lit room to see him digging deep into the bag, all eyes on him.

He watched in fascination as Mr. Kady reached into the bag and withdrew a large square box and handed it to his wife. It was embossed in gold and had the hand-woven pattern of an elephant adorned in gold coverings on its feet, head, and torso. The animal was set against a vivid crimson circle. The artwork was embossed on each side of the box; it was beautiful. Ram almost gasped out loud as Mrs. Kady opened the box. Inside was a series of progressively smaller boxes, each one nested inside another, until she had displayed a series of about half a dozen identical but smaller ones.

She gasped audibly and hugged him as she unveiled the gift. She was apparently as taken with the present as Ram was. It was, he thought, the most extraordinary thing he had ever seen.

Despite feeling like a spy, Ram held his position as Mr. Kady again dipped into the bag with gifts for the boys as well. For Chandra, it was a hand-made game called <u>Bagh Chal</u>, often referred to as Goat and Tiger in Nepal. It was a classic game of strategy and logic that was a favorite in Kathmandu. But this version was by far of much more superior quality than was found in most of the stores in town. Chandra beamed at his father as he clutched the game to his chest.

For Manu, it was a hand-carved game called <u>Pallanguli</u>. Manu smiled in delight and hugged his father tightly in thanks. Ram did not recall having ever seen such a reciprocal display of affection between this family. The boys ran off to their room with their games as Ram called from the kitchen to see if they might like some tea.

"Yes, Ram. That would be lovely," Mrs. Kady called back.

"Things have been good in my absence, Sarita?"

"Yes, Nabin. Ram has been incredibly efficient. Now, he is taking on more and more chores each week just on his own. He sees things that need to be done and just takes care of them – like asking about tea just now."

"Wonderful! He has begun his studies, as well?"

"Yes. I think he is struggling a bit, but he seems to love it."

"Then all is good."

Ram appeared just then with the tea service and poured them each a serving, leaving the pot on the tray.

"Welcome home, Mr. Kady." Ram bowed and hurried away.

*****

"Nabin?"

"Yes?"

"Did you not bring a gift for Ram, too?" Sarita spoke in a low voice.

"I…well…he is just the house boy, dear."

"In your absence, I think you will find he and the boys have become like friends. He has been working so hard. I saw him spying on us from the kitchen just now while you were handing out gifts. I think he may be feeling a bit left out."

"I just did not think to include him. I will take care of this now, though."

"Thank you, Nabin."

Nabin arose and left the room, returning to his seat as he concealed an elaborate handkerchief that had been in a spare bedroom down the hallway. He dropped it into the woven bag, then called for Ram. He came at once and stood by Mr. Kady's side.

"More tea, sir?"

"No, Ram. This is fine. Please, sit with us."

*****

Ram did as he was told, but sat erect and straight on the edge of a chair, not knowing what this might be about.

"Ram, I understand that you have been doing an excellent job in my time away."

"Thank you, sir."

"You may have noticed that I came back with presents for everyone. You, too."

Ram felt his heart leap. He watched with anticipation as Mr. Kady reached into the bag.

"This is for you, Ram."

Nabin handed the handkerchief to him and sat back as Ram accepted the offering. Ram knew immediately that this was no gift from India. He had seen the decorated cloth often when he had cleaned out the bedrooms during his daily routine. He did, to his credit, though, accept the gift with a smile and a bow. He stood and was overly effusive in his appreciation to his benefactor. Ram placed the handkerchief carefully on the counter in the kitchen, then returned to collect the tea service and clean it up before heading to bed.

He had been so hopeful that the warmer relationships he had begun to cultivate with Mrs. Kady and the boys would extend to Mr. Kady, too. But he could see he would never be more than a servant to him. He obviously had not brought him anything back from India, and Mrs. Kady had apparently stepped in to make it appear as if he had.

Ram felt his whole body sag in disappointment as he carried the cloth with him to bed. He would make sure it was displayed prominently in case Mr. Kady came around. He did not want him to know that he knew.

He was sure that this pain in his stomach would pass. After all, his relationships with everyone else had not changed; they were still intact. He would not let this one bad instance color it all. He would feel better in time. But tonight, he felt awful.

10.

A Mother's Touch

The time went by more quickly than Ram had anticipated. He, Chandra, and Manu had become good friends in the last few years. Though they were not true brothers, they often felt like brothers to Ram. He never let his new friendship with them interfere with the fact that he was still the house boy, but it sure made his life more enjoyable.

Mrs. Kady was still demanding of him, but she no longer made the unreasonable demands that had made his early days with them so painful. Ram loved being able to use his growing volume of English with her around the house. She always made it a point to commend him on his progress with it and offer minor corrections when he was just a tad off in his choice of words.

Mr. Kady, on the other hand, had soon reverted to the man that Ram had known from the beginning. His temper and tendency to express it at the slightest frustration was apparently just deeply ingrained in his personality. At least he was not as routinely disrespectful of Ram, as he had been in the beginning. It was generally just over nothing, really, in Ram's observations.

He was glad that he had grown up in such a calm and peaceful atmosphere as a young boy. He had never heard either of his parents ever raise their voices in anger, and certainly neither had ever smashed inanimate objects as a result. Both were still common sights in the Kady household. He found himself routinely comparing the difficult but calm life in the village to the more comfortable but chaotic life of the Kadys.

Ram often worried about the effect that this might have on the boys as they grew to be adults. Not only was it possibly inflicting emotional scarring on them, but it was also setting an example of behavior that might be passed along to the next generation of Kadys. Were they going to grow up to be like their father? Was this anger issue something that ran in the family?

He saw what it was doing to Mrs. Kady. She looked constantly on edge whenever he was around and had developed a nervous twitch in her eye. She tried to not let the boys see how it affected her, but she could not hide the deep fear in her eyes. Ram was sure this was the result of her husband's volatile unpredictability. He reasoned that if he just kept his head down, was respectful to him, and did everything that was asked of him, he would be spared. And lately, this had been the case.

His friendship with Chandra and Manu had branched out to some of the other kids at school, as well. The early days in the school had not been smooth sailing, though. Some of the kids had refused to share seats with Ram when they realized he was hired help. He often got teased about some of the words he used, as they were not common to the city and indicative of his village upbringing. They teased him about the same sets of clothes he wore. Some of the kids even remembered them being Chandra's old clothes and mocked him for it.

Now, merely by association with Chandra and Manu, Ram had begun to cultivate a small circle of friends at school. His command of English had helped, too. He was no longer referred to as the "village boy" – not even behind his back anymore.

Ram's education was blossoming, too; he began to excel in his classes now that his language skills gave him a greater understanding of the material. Chandra and Manu were still willing and available to help him, but as time went on, Ram was needing less and less of their assistance.

Ram had also become much more efficient in his responsibilities at the house, which gave him more time to do school work. Several other perks had just recently arisen, too. Chandra and Manu, at great personal risk, were sneaking extra food to Ram when they were sure no one was looking. They felt bad that he had to wait until all his chores were done before he could eat, and that what his parents portioned out for him was often lousy. They could see that he often went to bed still hungry, so they squirreled away what they could for him.

On occasions, they would even share a piece of chocolate or a sweet with him. This always brought a smile in his face. The taste of chocolate was like no other. He loved the burst of sensations it brought to his mouth. It was like a magic potion; just a small amount of those dark, sweet treats lightened up everything. That slightly sweet and bitter taste made him forget everything for few minutes and gave him a sense of relaxation like no other. This was a rare occasion, but he cherished every moment. Just the sight of chocolate made him salivate now.

In addition, when their parents were not around, they would let him watch television. Recently they had even started letting him observe them playing computer games. The electronic images fascinated Ram; he often found himself spending too much time with this instead of studying. He would stand right behind the brothers as they played soccer or cricket on the computer.

At times, he would get so immersed in the games that he would cheer as they scored a goal or won a cricket match. Chandra often had to remind him to not stay so close, as he was yelling directly in their ears. He would move back for few moments, but before they knew it, he would be right back over their shoulder. They had started getting comfortable with all this and just let him be.

Overall, though, Ram had to say he was happy. He still missed his family and life in Chandisthan from time to time, but he could not complain. Kathmandu had its allure, he guessed, but it was just not the same. As always, though, Ram made do with what he had.

However, a complication soon arose for Ram that he never, ever would have anticipated. One day, while playing a game with some of his classmates, Ram looked out across the playground and a young girl that caught his eye. He had never much noticed girls before, but this slender, black-haired beauty was hard to miss.

Her long black hair was carefully braided and she wore a bright yellow headband that made her stand out among all her friends. She had a small mole on her face and the dimples that formed when she smiled made her look like an angel. He could not help but just stand and stare at her.

To further complicate the situation, he discovered that she was the daughter of a family that lived just two doors down from the Kadys. He wondered how he had never noticed her at home before. But now, he could not get her out of his mind.

He saw her constantly, both at home and at school, and soon, he realized that he had become infatuated with her. He added extra trips as he did his chores in hopes of catching another glimpse of her as he passed by. He would jump on any excuse that would get him out of the house and toward her home.

She smiled slyly at him when he walked by her house with Chandra and Manu. Also, she always seemed to be sneaking peeks at Ram when he was in the yard playing with his friends, at school, and even in the hallways between classes. He thought it was no coincidence that she spent more and more time in the front yard of her house. Some days, Ram could hear her voice as he was chopping vegetables and would try to peek through the window, risking chopping his finger.

He was madly, deeply in love with the neighborhood princess. He longed to hear her voice and talk to her. He wanted to be close to her and just stare at those beautiful eyes all day. There were so many thoughts in his mind, but he could not gather enough courage to express those to her or anyone else. He had no idea how to proceed.

All he knew was that he could not get her out of his mind. He daydreamed about her when he worked, and his dreams at night were now filled with her. He supposed that he could ask Chandra or Manu for advice, but he was afraid that this would get out among his classmates and the taunting that he had just escaped from would begin anew. And maybe this time, since this involved a girl, Chandra and Manu would be among those teasing him.

After a week or so of this indecision and fretting over what to do, Ram came up with a plan. He would slip her a note at her home one morning as he went off to school. That way, she would know his feelings and if she was not of the same mind, then it would not be a big, public spectacle.

Ram struggled over what to say for a couple of days, writing and re-writing his declaration of love for her. When he was sure he had just the right words, he steeled himself to deliver it the next morning. Upon awakening, he purposely lingered over his morning chores so that he would finish up a bit later than usual. He told Chandra and Manu to go ahead without him; he would catch up as soon as he was finished, thus ensuring he would not be discovered.

The whole day went by and nothing happened. Ram watched for her all day, but each time he spied her, she just waved and smiled as normal, giving no indication that she had read his note. Maybe she was just not interested? That option felt devastating to Ram.

He worried and fretted all day, wondering, his mind anywhere but on his classes. At the end of the day, she still had said nothing. Ram plodded home with Chandra and Manu, his heart heavy and his mind a whirlwind of questions. An uncomfortable feeling of anxiety took over him. He went through his chores that night in a blind haze, just doing everything by rote, hardly having any conscious awareness of what it was he was doing.

Ram went to bed that night depressed and confused. He had crafted his note so thoroughly. What happened? Maybe she had not gotten it? Or, maybe she got it and his English was still too broken for her to understand it? Or, worst of all, maybe she was not interested. What was he thinking, slipping a love letter to a city girl? He wished he could go back in time and erase this whole day from existence. He felt like a complete fool for pouring his heart out in such a manner. She was from Kathmandu; maybe him being from a backward village was a problem.

He fell asleep, tossing and turning. The last thing Ram remembered before drifting off was that there was a short school break beginning tomorrow and he would not have to see her in school for a couple of days. That was good.

*****

Ram arose early to begin his regular household duties, feeling very unrested and dejected. He spent some extra time in meditation to clear his mind of all the noise from his apparent miscalculation.

Upon rising from his posture, he was feeling a bit better. Making the breakfast for the Kadys helped distract him from his concerns, as well, and by the time he had cleaned up the dishes, he was on the mend. Ram was about to begin checking all the rooms for trash and dirt when he heard Mrs. Kady calling to him from the living room.

"Yes, Ma'am?"

"Before you start on the sweeping, could I get you to run an errand for me?"

"Of course, Mrs. Kady."

"Please run down to the upholstery shop around the corner and take them this sample. Tell Mr. Bhandari that I want to use this pattern to recover the chairs in the dining room."

She handed Ram the small fabric swatch and he headed out the door, looking forward to a break in his normal routine. Until yesterday, he would have been excited for this opportunity to pass by his dream girl's house. He would have jumped at this chance to catch another glimpse of that smiling face.

Today, he was expressionless with a wandering mind. Ram was trying to forget about the girl and the note as he prepared to cross the road to make a more direct route to Mr. Bhandari's store. He walked briskly down the walk, feeling good as the sun shone on his face. He could hear the faint strains of music making their way through the neighborhood from a nearby house.

He turned to check for traffic on Maharajgungi Road when a hand came from nowhere, grabbing him by the collar of his coat and jerking him backward off his feet.

Ram cried out in surprise and shock, his coat and shirt choking him as he flew in reverse. He came to a stop painfully, in a heap on his rear, still having no idea what had happened. He fell backwards onto his back in the dirt, looking up into the face of a highly irate and screaming woman.

Her teeth were clenched together and her face was a red from anger. The nerves in her neck and the side of her face looked like they were ready to pop. She held a crumpled piece of paper in one hand and was shaking it wildly in his face. She so overcome with anger that she could not bring herself to speak clearly.

In her other hand, she held a thick stalk of bamboo. It was the kind of bamboo stalk that was used in the village to herd animals. Ram raised his arms just in time to ward off the blows that began to rain down on him from his assailant. He tried to get up to run, but the woman kicked his leg to bring him back in the ground. He was still utterly confused as he cowered and balled himself smaller for protection.

"You servant dog!" the woman bellowed. "How dare you look upon my daughter in such a way!" Without a pause in the beating, she continued. "Who do you think gave you the right to lay your dirty eyes on my innocent daughter?"

Ram was busy trying to simultaneously protect himself, crawl away, and figure out what this was about. He heard the woman's screaming, but her words were not registering in his head. The woman grasped him again so he could not escape. In doing so, she threw the mangled paper at his feet so she could continue her assault.

Despite the pain and humiliation of the beating, Ram managed to see that the paper at his feet was, in fact, the note he had slipped under the gate to the neighbor girl he had become infatuated with. Apparently, this was her mother, and she was none too happy about it. The girl, it would seem, had never received the note; it had been intercepted by her mother. That was why there had been no response from her. For a split second, he was happy that he might not have been so wrong about his feelings.

"You animal! I will whip you like the despicable cur you are! You dare to insult her with your words and looks! I should break your hands for writing those words to my daughter!"

Ram could not get away from her firm hold. Even though he had managed to turn his back to her, the lashings from the bamboo were doing a lot of damage to him. He felt as if he could take no more. He pleaded with her to stop and cried out for help, but there seemed to be no one coming to his aid.

Suddenly, the blows ceased, and Ram felt himself being lifted up and away from the melee. A large body now stood between him and the irate neighbor woman. Through his pain and fear, he looked up to see that it was Mr. Kady. He was sure he was hallucinating.

The woman fell back as Mr. Kady pushed her away. He snatched away the bamboo rod, snapping it firmly over his knee and tossing the broken pieces into the gutter. Ram got to his knees and bent over with his head near the pavement. Every part of his battered body seemed to cry out.

"What is the meaning of this, Bhagya?"

The woman went on in some detail, repeating to him what Ram had done and how it had brought shame to her daughter and the family name.

"How dare he? How dare *you*, you ignorant cow!"

Bhagya shrank back, stung by his words. By now, a small group of neighbors had begun to collect and she felt all their eyes on her. She looked around, trying to find some support among them as she panted.

"The boy is under *my* employ. If you have a problem with something he had done, you come and see me or Sarita. Do I make myself clear?"

She remained silent, still reeling from Nabin's defense of Ram.

"He is just a young boy. He is new to the city and still learning its ways. He sometimes does not know what he is doing, but this? This is unacceptable. You come to me in the future. I will not be so understanding or kind toward you in the future if there is a repeat of such behavior on your part! Again, *do I make myself clear?*"

Bhagya finally looked Nabin in the eyes and simply nodded before she turned and slunk away back to her home. The neighbors, one-by-one, went their own way, leaving Nabin and Ram alone. Just as all the commotion came to an end, Nabin looked up to see Sarita running toward them, with Chandra and Manu close behind.

Nabin knelt down to Ram and looked him over. Sarita finally caught up to them and her hands flew to her mouth as she looked at the bruised and bloodied Ram, aghast at what had happened.

"Ram?" Nabin spoke to him softly and in a gentle manner that Ram had no idea that the man was even capable of. "Are you okay? Can you stand?"

Ram looked up at him, tears flowing, and nodded slowly. He got to his feet with Nabin's assistance. Even with all the welts and cuts and bruises, he seemed to be intact. Ram took a few tentative steps and, though they were stiff and awkward, he seemed to be able to move. He was thankful that no bones had been broken.

He felt humiliated, but at the same time, was overcome with gratitude that Mr. Kady had rushed to his defense. In a thousand years, he would never had thought such a thing possible.

"Sarita, draw a bath. Get some ointments and bandages out. I will help Ram get home. Then, you can get him cleaned up and into bed. I will explain everything to you later."

Ram was sure he must have been hearing things. This could not possibly be the same man who lost his temper at home so easily, who threw things against the floor and walls in frustration. Mrs. Kady hurried back to their house and he limped along with Mr. Kady and the boys.

Both Chandra and Manu looked at him in horror and shock. He was sure they had never seen such a sight. He heard what Mr. Kady had told the woman. He had not thought that what he had done was so egregious, but apparently, there were rules in the city of which he had no knowledge.

Ram hobbled along and Mr. Kady supported him with one arm. Once they had made it home, Mrs. Kady showed him to a bath that he had, up to this point, had no access to, other than to clean it up. She had a clean set of his clothes lying nearby, as well as cloths he could use to bathe his wounds with.

"Take your time, Ram. When you are done, I can help put some ointment on your cuts and other injuries. It will help speed the healing."

Ram just nodded as he began to cry again. They were not tears of pain, though. He was ashamed and embarrassed. He was here to serve the Kadys, not the other way around.

After a careful bath, Ram dressed himself and wandered out into the hallway and toward the kitchen, where he heard voices. Mrs. Kady arose quickly as he entered and motioned for him to follow her. Ram hung his head and did as instructed. She opened a door to a small room that Ram had never been in before and had him sit on a nearby sofa. She busied herself with some tubes, powders, and bandages.

"Mr. Kady filled me in, Ram. I am so sorry this happened. I feel responsible for having asked you to go on that errand."

"No, Mrs. Kady. It was all me. I just had no idea…."

"It's okay. Just relax. Bhagya, the woman who beat you? She is not well-liked in the neighborhood. This is just how she is."

Ram closed his eyes as Mrs. Kady worked the homemade ointment onto his wounds with the gentle and practiced touch of a mother. A tear slowly rolled out from the burning sensation as the ointment touched his raw skin. The burn dulled the sharp pain he had been feeling.

A sea of emotions washed over him. The homemade ointment had a familiar scent of marigold and mint. His mom used to prepare the same ointment anytime he fell as a child. Her gentle touch and this magic ointment seemed to heal any wounds in no time. Now, Mrs Kady had the same ointment. He wondered if his mom had told Mrs. Kady about the ointment at the village.

His mind was racing with all these thoughts and his heart was melting with all the new emotions from the Kadys. Unable to understand what he was feeling, he just listened to her as she finished up and then took great care applying bandages over the more serious of his open cuts.

"Ram, Kathmandu is still new to you. This is not Chandisthan, where all the people are so kind and understanding. As you grow older here, you will learn this. And what you did? It was not so awful. It was just impulsive and, unfortunately, you picked the wrong place."

Sarita smiled to herself, remembering the first time a boy in her class had passed her a note. It was a rite of passage and it still was a fond memory for her.

"If there is something like this again, come see me or Mr. Kady. I know there have been some rough times here, especially when you first arrived to us, but things are different now. You have done a wonderful job for us. Come talk to us if you have questions about anything."

Ram looked at her with tears in his eyes. It was almost too much for him to take in. The kindness and protection that the Kadys had afforded him in this misadventure filled his heart with gratitude. He had seen his relationship with Mrs. Kady warming over the years, but having Mr. Kady step in today was totally unexpected.

He nodded to her and thanked her profusely as he eased himself off the couch. He wanted to thank them, but he could barely say a word without crying.

"What about the cleaning today? And dinner?"

"Ram, just rest. We can manage for a few days until you are feeling better. Follow me."

Ram did as she asked and found himself led to a bedroom that he had never seen anyone use since he had been here. She opened the door and Ram saw that the bed was covered with crisp, clean sheets and a light blanket. She motioned for him to enter and Ram just looked at her in puzzlement.

"Rest here. I will come check on you later to make sure all your bandages are still good and do not need to be changed."

She smiled and walked out, pulling the door shut behind her. Ram was left alone, staring at the bed. He had never slept in a bed before – not a real bed like this, anyway. He touched the sheets, then sat on the edge of the bed and just cried. *It was a miracle*, Ram thought.

He lay back carefully on the clean linens, taking care to not disturb the dressings. The bed smelled like flowers and laundry detergent and had a calming effect on him. The pillows were soft and feathery, unlike his pillow made with old clothes. He looked around the bed and could not understand why there were so many pillows.

As he lay down, he could feel the tender spots on his body and he winced. The herbal smell from the ointment still brought him a mixed feeling of relaxation and homesickness. He could not find a position to be comfortable in. It seemed like his body hurt everywhere and every time he turned, he found a new area that hurt.

Tossing and turning, he kept debating if he would have been better off staying in his village, or if this life in the city was worth everything he had been through. At least now, it seemed like he had a loving family with him no matter where he was.

He was soon asleep. In his dreams, there was no pain, just the overwhelming emotions of what this family had become to him. He now knew they truly would be there for him in times of real need.

11.

House Boy

With each year that went by, Ram found himself feeling more and more at home – not only with the Kady's, but in sprawling Kathmandu, too. He was getting used to hustle and bustle of the city, along with its pollution and the crowds. He was now comfortable taking the bus by himself and walking to far ends of the city, looking for the best fruits and vegetable for the Kadys.

His English was improving by leaps and bounds, but he still found himself struggling with other classes in school. At age sixteen, Ram was only in the sixth grade and he was often reprimanded for not finishing his homework on time. He had to repeat fifth grade, as he struggled with the standardized tests. Like many children, it had less to do with Ram's ability to learn the material than his dedication and discipline at home.

Ever since Chandra and Manu had given Ram more access to television, his fascination with it had become a serious distraction. When he spent what little free time he had watching television, it only meant his study time took a back seat and was often completely abandoned.

Mrs. Kady sometimes had to remind Ram to be more thorough with his chores, as he sometimes rushed through them so he can watch TV. He often asked the Kadys if they wanted to eat a little earlier so he could finish his chores by the 9 P.M. TV show. This drove Mrs. Kady crazy in the beginning. She would constantly remind him that he was there to work, and *not* to watch TV.

Ram still remembered the time when he was peeking through the door, watching a soccer match. He thought no one noticed him when Mrs. Kady came from right behind him, grabbed him by the ears, and dragged him to the kitchen. She screamed at him so loudly that the kids had to ask her to keep it down so the neighbors would not wake up.

She wanted to make sure that Ram understood that she was serious about the rules. She also wanted to send a clear message that Ram was *not* a part of the family and did *not* get to do everything that the boys did.

Things had changed a lot since then. Ram had assimilated more into the Kadys' family. There was still no doubt that he was the hired help and does not get to do everything the boys do. However, Mrs. Kady was more lenient with Ram now. Now, when Ram asked if they could eat a little earlier so he can finish up by nine, Mrs. Kady just smiled and joked with her family, saying, "The King cannot miss a single minute of his TV show, so let's all go eat!"

More relaxed TV time also meant that his studying time, which had to wait until all the chores were completed, would get cut into at times. This led to him not always having all his assignments completed, and thus, being reprimanded by his teachers. It was a vicious cycle that Ram had found himself in from time to time.

Even though the altercation he had incurred at the hands of the neighborhood woman, Bhagya, had been demoralizing at the time, it had held a silver lining for him in the end. He had not won the affections of the girl, but the experience had been so shocking and traumatic for Ram that he just decided to focus on what he saw as his new family.

He did not know if the episode had been the turning point for Mr. Kady or if it was just coincidental. But ever since that day, he had been a different man. Ram still saw Mr. Kady get frustrated and annoyed from time to time, but the explosiveness and uncontrollable displays of temper seemed to have vanished. The best part of this was how it had flowed down to his family. Mrs. Kady seemed more relaxed and the nervous tics that she had once displayed were no more. There was more laughter and a warmer atmosphere in the house.

Both Chandra and Manu seemed in better spirits when their father was around, as well. Much like their mother, Ram used to see a veil of unease and uncertainty come over the boys when their father arrived home from work, like they were just waiting for the bomb to go off. But since what Ram now referred to as "the episode", all seemed much improved. Mr. Kady was closer to his family now, too, exhibiting signs of great emotional attachment that had, until now, been non-existent.

As for Ram? He was still the house boy; that had not changed. But somehow, Ram felt he had attained a different status. There was not something tangible that he could really point to, but just this feeling he got as he went about his chores and interacted with the family. He was closer to Chandra and Manu now, and if someone from the outside had seen them, they might have sworn all were brothers.

Overall, it was just more pleasant to work in an environment filled with smiles and laughter versus a place overshadowed with anxiety and nerves. The Kadys had now begun to entertain more guests in their home and Ram was pleased to be a big part of making them feel comfortable. His improving English skills made Ram more outgoing and confident, and he often took the Kadys' guests on tours of the neighborhood like they were old friends from Chandisthan.

This was not even something that the Kadys had asked of him. Ram had just stepped up and offered. He seemed to mingle so well with the visitors and everyone seemed so drawn to him that it just became a natural progression. Mrs. Kady beamed in appreciation at all the compliments she received about Ram. To him, it did not seem like a big deal. He loved it.

*****

Mr. Kady's company in Kathmandu had expanded dramatically in the last six months, so he had taken on a whole new range of responsibilities there. It also brought him an increase in his salary, and he came one day to announce that he had secured a new piece of land nearby on which a new house was to be built.

Everyone seemed wildly excited about it, though Ram, looking around the current house, could not quite see what might be wrong with the one they had. He figured it was just something he would never understand, being from a small village.

However, Ram soon joined the excitement when Mr. Kady revealed that he would have his own room. It took him no time to get lost in his dream world, imagining the details of his future room. He could only imagine how happy his parents would be when he would tell them all about it on the next holiday.

The lot was just a short walk from the house, and Ram wandered over during his free time just to observe the progress. After the first few trips, he decided to measure how far the lot was from their current house. One day, he brought a pen and paper with him during the trip and recorded how many steps there were and how long the trip took him. He stopped at every intersection and jotted down the number of steps. At the end of the trip, he added up the steps to get to the total.

Ram beamed with pride and excitement at what he had been able to do. Any time after that day, when they had a visitor or when anyone asked how far the new house was, he jumped with excitement and shouted out:

"It is 1,937 steps away and takes fifteen minutes to get there, but twenty minutes to come back since it is slightly uphill."

Most people would just laugh and continue their conversation with the Kadys. On rare occasions, if someone asked him how he knew the exact time and steps, Ram's excitement would reach a different high. He loved being able to tell people how he had recorded the time and steps personally.

He had never seen a real house being built before. The whole process was interesting and exciting for him. Mr. Kady had brought home the plans for the new place and he spent many hours with his family, showing them all the rooms and explaining all the features. Ram would usually stand by the door and listen to the family discussion, curious if there had been any changes to his room. To Ram, though, the building plans just looked like a weird drawing with lines and figures all over the place, laid out randomly. How was this to become a house? It seemed impossible.

Ram watched the workers move in a sort of coordinated dance as they moved about the site. It was so different from anything he had ever seen or done that he found himself mesmerized. He usually sat by the construction site and kept record of everything that was brought to the site. He was excited to be able to use his literary skills any chance he got. Little Ram looked like a contractor, walking around with a notebook and pencil, keeping notes. He would neatly write down descriptions of the trucks and what they delivered.

Red truck, delivered one truckload of sand at 11:22 A.M.

Delivery team from Jay's Construction delivered seven bags of cement at 1:15 P.M.

His notebook was filled with details like these every day. He loved showing his notes to the Kadys in the evening. Ram found himself fully immersed in this fast-moving environment. He enjoyed maintaining a detailed record of everything that happened around the site, but he wanted to do more.

He saw the workers putting up walls and filling pillars with concrete. It amazed him how the cement attached the bricks together. He was curious about almost everything that happened at the site and wanted to learn, rather than just watch.

On a whim, he spoke to one of the workers to see if he could help. Building something looked like fun, and on some level, Ram thought that if they had more help, the house would go up sooner. Then, his new room would be done sooner, as well. He could not stop thinking about his new room. *His own room.* It still sounded like a dream to him.

The worker laughed and said as long as his foreman did not object, they could always use some more hands – especially hands they did not have to pay for.

The foreman had no objections. Ram pitched in where he could, usually moving bricks around or carrying bags of sand for the workers.

He also ran messages back and forth for them so they could keep building without interruption and ran errands into town for small batches of supplies.

Over time, the formless backbone of the new house began to come together and take shape. From what had seemed to just be nothing, suddenly, rooms began to emerge and he could see an actual house appearing before him. The ground floor was complete and the workers were starting on the second floor already.

The house went up quickly. Ram was nearly bouncing off the walls in excitement as he helped with the moving of the household goods to the new location. He stared in awe as he walked into the empty shell, amazed at what a seemingly random pile of building materials had become. As amazing as the Kadys' old house had been to him upon his arrival in Kathmandu, this new one was even more so.

It was not that it was so much larger or more elaborate or overwhelming in design, but more that he felt a real connection to it since he had helped in the construction of it. The homes he had known in Chandisthan had been so simple that he had no idea such places for ordinary families even existed.

As he had gotten involved, Ram had become more curious and fascinated by the process and he felt, at least on some level, that a part of him was incorporated here. After a few days, when all the goods had finally been relocated from the former residence, Ram waited impatiently to see where his own room was to be.

It would be his first real room just to himself. He eagerly followed Mr. Kady down a hallway as he led Ram to his new space. He was surprised as they walked by a lot of the empty rooms, sure that one of them was to be his. Finally, Mr. Kady stopped at a small door that led to an enclosure under the stairs, located between one of the bathrooms and the kitchen.

He opened the triangular-shaped door and Ram peered in to see the interior. It was not exactly what he had been expecting, but the Kadys had done a nice job of setting up his sleeping pad along one wall, which allowed adequate space for Ram's books and other things from school.

It was not the bedroom that Ram had pictured in his mind when he had first heard that he was to have his own private bedroom, but it was his own space. There was even adequate headroom for him to be able to do his daily meditations. Ram, though not exactly thrilled, was happy.

He had to remind himself once again of his role in this family. Despite how his relationship with Mr. and Mrs. Kady had improved dramatically since he had arrived, he was still not a family member. He smiled broadly and thanked them profusely for what they had done to provide him with his own room.

Having come from a simple background made Ram even more appreciative, and having a bathroom close by was good. Also, having the kitchen right there was nice, too, since this was where he was now spending most of his working hours.

In all of Ram's life, he had tried to always be grateful for anything that came his way, regardless of whether it matched up with his expectations. He set about rearranging his new space so that it was more efficient and made the best use of the limited space before setting off to familiarize himself with the rest of the new house.

Ram soon learned his way around in the new house. It was much better laid out, and this made his chores less cumbersome. Both Mrs. Kady and the boys seemed happier in the new place. Mr. Kady, though not home as much anymore, looked pleased, too.

School continued to chug along for Ram as well. Though his English skills were now very good, he continued to struggle with many of his other subjects. It was not that Ram could not do the work, exactly, but more that he just got bored easily and began having trouble concentrating in class. He just could not seem to see how all the things they were teaching had any real, practical application for him.

He had spent so much time in manual labor with the Kadys that he was finding himself more drawn to physical labor, rather than what his teachers seemed to value in school. One of the big goals that Ram had set for himself when he had left Chandisthan was to have a good command of English. At this point, Ram felt proud that he had accomplished that. He had never really thought ahead to what he might want to do with his life once he had done this, but there was nothing in his lessons so far that had struck him as to a path he might follow now.

Ram had a rudimentary knowledge of mathematics that had come in handy with some of his household chores, as well as when he had helped the workers as they built the new house, but nothing else seemed to him to be of much use. He was getting to the age, though, when he needed to be making decisions in this regard.

He thought Mr. Kady was some sort of designer or engineer, but this was just a guess. He certainly seemed to be making a good salary, but Ram had seen how stressful his job was. He was not sure it was worthwhile to live like that just to have money and nice things.

Certainly, when he had begun this path, this had been on his mind. He had seen the people in Pokhara and all that they seemed to have. This had made him want to strive for more. But if this was the price he had to pay for that level of life, Ram was not sure it was for him. He was sure there must be another way to get there.

It was just recently that Mr. Kady had seemed more relaxed and calm. His early days around the man were hideous and frightful, and he remembered how he had taken out his frustration on his family. Ram did not want that to happen to him.

Besides, he was sure that Mr. Kady had completed an extensive education to do his job. As much as Ram had enjoyed parts of his education, he was not too keen on spending years and years in a classroom. If only he had some clear-cut idea of what it was he wanted to do. He had surely had his fill of being a house boy. It was not overly strenuous work, but it was not anything he wanted to do for any longer than he absolutely had to. It was a means to an end.

He had taken on this role to get an education, but now that he had seen what a traditional education required in terms of dedication and discipline, Ram felt stuck. He knew in his heart that without a more formal education, he would be relegated to the role he had. So, how was he to advance beyond domestic servitude or returning to the farming life he had left behind in Chandisthan? Ram pondered this dilemma constantly while he was cleaning the Kadys' house or making meals, but it only made his head hurt.

Ram finally turned to his meditations for some answers. In all aspects of his life, this had been where he had gone for solutions to problems. It was a slow and long-term process, but Ram was sure if he could clear his mind and focus on this issue when he was meditating, his path would become evident. Having his own room now helped.

Despite missing the company of Chandra and Manu from time to time, Ram knew the solitude his private room gave him now would be necessary. Through sheer willpower, he forced himself to leave behind his fascination with the television and the boys' computer games. They had been an interesting diversion at the time, but for him to get clear on his future, Ram needed to divest himself of such distractions.

When he first started on this new path, Ram was frustrated and impatient, as his mind was filled with the chatter of what his life had become here in Kathmandu. The noise, the modern conveniences, the hordes of people everywhere – he realized now that they had all become hurdles for him to overcome.

And perhaps, Ram thought one night as he closed his eyes to go to sleep, this was needed for him to truly focus on what it was he wanted out of his life. One of the great lessons he recalled that his father had ingrained in him from a young age was that truly noble and worthwhile goals never came without obstacles.

Whether it was a farmer overcoming weather and poor soil conditions or a Buddhist monk tempted by the secular world, all men who achieved great things had to rise above their personal challenges. Ram was suddenly calmed as these thoughts came to him. He realized that he had been fighting against all the bumps in the road that he had encountered since arriving in Kathmandu. Instead, he should have seen them as lessons.

He should have ridden out the waves of the ocean instead of trying to plow through them by sheer force of strength. He certainly had the physical and emotional bruises to show him that this had been futile.

12.

Home

Once Ram had this revelation, his mind's background chatter went silent. The focus and clarity he had known from his practices as a young boy returned – *just like that*.

That is not to say, though, that the solution to Ram's dilemma was obvious. As he became clearer on his purpose and his intention, the voice that kept coming to Ram told him that he should go home.

Each time the picture of Chandisthan entered Ram's visions in this way, he felt confused. How was returning to Chandisthan going to make his path obvious? He had been going back there annually for the fall festival—it had been part of the agreement with the Kadys—but nothing had been clarified for him on these visits.

It was always a pleasure to be back in the simple surroundings that he had grown up with, to see his childhood friends and to reunite with his parents. When he had left for Kathmandu, Ram was not aware of this as being part of the arrangement, and he was relieved that the fear he had internalized about never seeing his parents again had been lifted.

There was something different about his simple village. It had none of the amenities of the city, and yet, he felt most at peace when he was home in Chandisthan. He loved the fact that he could walk through the whole village. Even more, he knew almost everyone, and if he did not know someone, chances were they would know him.

People would stop and ask him, "Aren't you Ram, the kid who lives in Kathmandu?" Being able to talk to people as he walked through the village always brought a smile to his face. Chandisthan never seemed to change much. Well, there were little changes here and there as certain neighbors expanded their agricultural efforts or as longtime neighbors passed away. But overall, Ram thought it was nice to always return to the same place he had always known so well.

His friends would gather around, anxious to hear of what Kathmandu was like. Most of them had never been farther away from the village than Khudi Bazaar, much less as far as Pokhara. They sat wide-eyed as Ram entertained them with the stories of his experiences there, even his misadventures with the Kadys or his run-in with Bhagya, the belligerent neighbor woman. The younger children gasped in disbelief as he told the latter tale, thinking he must be trying to scare them. *Surely, no one on the planet was this nasty!*

They were impressed with Ram's new command of English, which seemed to get better with each of his pilgrimages back. Likewise, some of the older kids, those closer to Ram's own age, always pointed out how much older he seemed. He usually brushed off the comment by saying it was probably just because of the pollution in the city.

Ram thought on this observation when he had time to himself in the village. This had not really occurred to him when he was away. Everyone in Kathmandu seemed so far ahead of him in so many ways. But back here in the village, as he mingled and talked with his old friends, he could see what they meant. He had seen so much of the world outside of Chandisthan that most of them would never know, and he began to view himself in a different light.

He supposed they might be right. He was not sure if that was good or bad. Despite all the opportunities he had been afforded in Kathmandu, in a lot of ways, he sometimes envied them knowing nothing beyond the immediate perimeter of Chandisthan.

Being back home to see his parents was always the highlight of the trips for Ram, though. The festival activities were wonderful, but reconnecting with his mother and father was what he really looked forward to. The last few years had not been especially kind to them, but despite all the ups and downs, they looked well. Ram regaled them with his tales of his years away as well, but he never passed along the less than positive experiences. He never wanted them to worry about him more than they probably already did.

The festival season was a big time for tourists in the Annapurna Range, as well, and the tea houses in and around Khudi Bazaar were usually filled to the brim. Ram was excited to make the short walk there, too, to show off his new improved English skills. For several years, the visitors were just new faces to Ram, but then, one year, he looked across the courtyard in one of the tea houses that was frequented most by Americans. He was not sure, but the longer he looked, the more positive Ram was that there was a familiar face.

He walked toward the smiling man, whose brown beard had now begun to go gray a bit. The man was engaged in a conversation with one of the Sherpas over a pot of tea and he did not see Ram right away. Ram continued and just as he was nearing the man's table, the American looked up and locked eyes with Ram. The recognition was immediate.

The man excused himself from his conversation with the guide and offered his hand to Ram.

"Is it really you?"

"Afraid it is. Ram, isn't it?"

Ram was astonished that the man remembered him. It was the kind and generous man from years ago that had given him the book that had set him on a path to understanding English.

"It is, sir. Mr. Garrison, right?"

"It is. That's quite a memory you have, considering all of us who pass through here."

The man offered Ram a seat at his table and Ram sat.

"I will never forget you, Mr. Garrison. I still have the book you gave me, *The Old Man and the Sea*."

"Wow! That scruffy old book I left on my last trip?"

"Yes, sir. I love that book."

"Great! I can see your English has improved a lot. I wish my Nepali was as good as your English. The book has helped you?"

Ram laughed and entertained the man for a long time, letting him know how the book had led him to Kathmandu and all that had happened to him since he had last met him here. The man ordered another pot of tea and talked with Ram for a long time, until the sun was beginning its descent and Ram had to excuse himself so he could get home in time for dinner with his parents.

"Wonderful to see you again, Mr. Garrison."

"You, too, Ram. Take care and good luck with your studies."

Ram waved and began his walk back home. It was, he thought as he walked, odd running into the man again. He knew Americans often made multiple trips to Nepal, but still. The voice had said to go home. That was all. Go home. He had no idea what the significance of this was, but he was sure there was something behind it. *Did this chance reunion mean something, based on the message?*

The rest of his time in the village was uneventful. It was relaxing and peaceful, but otherwise, nothing of note occurred. Before he knew it, his time was up and the Kadys had arrived to take him back to Kathmandu.

Ram pondered this trip more deeply than he normally did on the ride back. Each time, going back to Kathmandu became harder and harder. It was not that he was unhappy there. Just the opposite. Though not a family member, the Kadys treated him well. More than well, actually, considering he was just their house boy. He was looking forward to seeing Chandra and Manu again, but there was something nagging at him that he could not figure out.

If all of this is going so well, then why does this voice in my meditation keep telling me to go home?

There was certainly nothing for him there if he wanted to get more out of his life than picking up where his father might leave off one day. *So, what was it?* The harder he thought, the more elusive the answer seemed. Ram finally shook his head and just let it go. He was sure it would come to him eventually.

Mrs. Kady turned in her seat to hear of his time back home, as had become the pattern on the rides back to Kathmandu. Mr. Kady peppered him with questions, too. They both seemed truly interested in his time away from them.

Ram smiled and talked with them easily and happily. It was such a stark contrast to that first ride to Kathmandu. The long ride flew by, as his mind was filled with anticipation and happiness now, as opposed to the anxiety and uncertainty just a few years earlier.

Ram popped out of the Land Rover as Chandra and Manu ran to meet them, hugging him as they laughed together. Mr. and Mrs. Kady smiled at the reunion, looking at each other and wondering how they had ever gotten along without Ram.

The house, in an odd way, seemed to be becoming more like home to Ram than where he had grown up with his parents. Part of him understood that since he was now spending much more time here than in Chandisthan, but it was also unsettling. Deep in his heart, he just did not feel like he fit in in Kathmandu. He headed to his room after the long drive to meditate on all the conflicting thoughts that were swirling in his mind. He also wanted to get to bed early, so that he could be well-rested prior to beginning his regular routine.

Ram arose early, as he always did to get a jump on the day. Everything went as it normally did, including another day at school, but he was still no clearer on what it was that he was that he was to do in the long run. The days turned into weeks and the weeks into months. Though Ram was happy with his life, he knew he could not do this forever. Other than mingling with his friends at school, as well as with Chandra and Manu, Ram felt he was being pulled apart, emotionally.

The girl that he had become infatuated with was suddenly no longer at the school, and Ram discovered one day that the family had abruptly left the neighborhood. He had long ago erased any more thoughts of her from his mind, not wanting a repeat experience from her mother. But it was odd that one day they were there, and the next, they were not.

Despite Mrs. Kady's assurance that he could come to them with anything, Ram thought this was a subject better left alone. The Kadys were not friends of the family, and since Mr. Kady's strong defense of him, there had been little, if any, activity seen from the house just down the street.

Ram kept his ears open, though, just out of curiosity. Sure enough, one day, he overheard some other neighbors passing along gossip about them. Apparently, the mother had lashed out at others since that day with Ram. She severely injured another boy and she had been hospitalized by the local authorities for being "unsound of mind".

Ram thought back to that day and how Mrs. Kady had mentioned that she had a history of such behavior. From what Ram had overheard, the father had packed up his children and left Kathmandu once she had been released to go and stay with relatives in Janakpur, near the border of India.

Due to her well-known behavior in Kathmandu, her husband had been given the alternative of criminal proceedings if they remained in Kathmandu. So, they just left the area, never to return. Ram had no idea if this was true or not, as the locals constantly bandied about wild and sometimes unbelievable stories about their neighbors. Some of it ended up being factual, but Ram also knew that most of it was just idle talk. He hoped for the girl's sake that this was the case, as it seemed that would be a horrible burden to live with growing up.

Perhaps her father had just found better employment elsewhere and they had quietly relocated. The Kadys said they were not generally well-liked, anyway, and this made more sense to him that the tale being told across neighborhood fences. Ram would say a prayer for her, just in case.

This was about the only real incident of note for Ram. School ground along. He was feeling no differently about his education than he had when he went back to Chandisthan for the festival.

He liked his friends and was coming to almost enjoy his responsibilities at the Kadys, but still knew this could not last. He was beginning to feel a strong sense of boredom creep in and he felt himself coming to yet another crossroad in his young life. He needed more, and wanting to move toward it was like an itch that had gotten under his skin and would not let him go.

Ram continued his meditation practices, and had even gotten Chandra and Manu interested in trying it for themselves. *What a surprise!* It was another drastic change from the days he was teased as "little Buddha". Ram did not feel knowledgeable enough to instruct them, but he certainly did his best to give them the basics. They seemed to take to it immediately, and it pleased Ram to see them incorporate it as a regular part of their day.

His own meditations, while calming and peaceful amid the hectic city, were not moving Ram any closer to an answer to his future. The message that kept coming back to him, over and over, was the same: go home. It was still as baffling to him as it had been from the beginning. He never gave up, though. Surely, it would come to him eventually.

*****

The remainder of the year passed without any significant incident, and before Ram knew it, his break to go back to Chandisthan for the fall festival had come once more. He rode along in silence with the Kadys this time, hoping that this year would be the one in which a revelation was bestowed on him.

The Kadys were normally talkative on these trips, but even they could sense a seriousness not seen before in Ram. They respected his demeanor and dropped him off with a simple farewell, promising to see him again in a week for his return to Kathmandu.

Ram could not explain it, but in his heart, he had this feeling that he might not see the Kadys again. It made no sense, but all the same, the feeling was there. He watched as the cloud of dust trailed behind the bouncing form of the Land Rover as it disappeared over the faraway ridge. Ram finally turned away from the road and walked toward his parents' home, feeling both relieved and sad.

The time of the festival would be much the same as it had always been, but this year, several new experiences awaited Ram. He just did not know it yet.

13.

The Gift

Ram arrived home to find his parents looking much older and frailer than he had remembered them. It had just been one year since the last holiday visit, but they looked so much different. The year, Ram's father said, had been one of the hardest for them. His health was limiting his ability to do as much farming as he once had.

Everyone in the village had struggled with their crops due to a combination of harsh summer weather, unexpected fall winds, and just inexplicable bad luck. His father, Ram noticed, was now using a walking stick a bit to get around. He no longer had a strong gait; he hunched forward and walked slowly. His mother was not looking any better. She had a nagging cough that never seemed to let up.

Ram was shocked at what he had come home to. Maybe this is what the voice had meant. It was time for him to come home to take care of his aging parents. It was not a bad thing, just unexpected. He figured it was the least he could do after all they had done and sacrificed for him.

He sat with his parents that night and shared the same simple meal with them that he looked forward to all year: his mother's curry lentils. With all that Kathmandu had to offer, no one there had ever come close to reproducing this savory treat.

He cleaned up for his mother as they rested by the fire. Ram had no solid background in farming, though, other than the bits and pieces he had seen when working with his father. And obviously, there would be no trek to Pokhara any time soon.

Ram fell fast asleep following his prayers to bring him a resolution to this new problem. The night passed silently as the family slept. However, when Ram woke up, he would get all the clarity he had been seeking for so long.

*****

Ram arose very early; it had become habitual from his long tenure with the Kadys. The sun was just peeking over the mountains as he looked over his parents' home, toward Gangapurna. It was one of the lesser-known major peaks of the Annapurnas, but remained Ram's favorite. It did not have the distinctive shape that so many tourists clamored here to see, but to Ram, it was special.

It was going to be sunny, but chilly. Fall seemed to be giving way to winter too soon. The festival was to begin in full that day and Ram smiled as he anticipated the events. It was a time in which he could reconnect with his friends and find out what had been going on both in the village and their lives.

Ram bundled himself with his heavy coat that he had carried with him since he had left to go to Kathmandu. He quickly checked on his parents before leaving. Both his father and mother were still sound asleep; his mother's cough blessedly had calmed, letting her rest. Ram pulled the covers over them and smiled, then turned to go.

He walked just across the village square and immediately ran into three of his boyhood friends, who also came back annually for the festival. Ram did not know where they had gone these days, only that, like himself, they were looking for more out of their lives than to be farmers in Chandisthan.

They waved heartily to Ram. He hustled over to greet them as the sun finally rose fully into the morning sky. Despite the long separations between them, Ram reveled in the fact that it was like no time at all had passed.

"Ram! Look at you! How have you been?"

"And you, my friends! You all look so strong and fit. Where are you, these days? What are you doing?"

They sat on the benches in the square that had been there as long as Ram could remember. His friend, Adarsh, handed him a cup of chhaang. Apparently, they had started celebrating the festival already. Ram accepted the drink and they all toasted their good fortune. Ram was not a drinker, but the fermented rice tasted tart and sour on his tongue and he smiled.

As they talked and exchanged stories, Ram discovered that they had gone to the Middle East and found jobs as laborers. They had heard rumors that there was much money to be made there, as more and more Western influences poured in and the demand for workers in construction far outweighed the supply of local people. Ram listened with rapt attention, amazed at the amounts of money that his friends were being paid. It seemed inconceivable, yet he knew they would not lie to him.

They were sending a lot of money back to their families to help support them when times were tough, as had been the case for the last few seasons. Even so, they could still live well, better than they could ever hope to here.

Ram began to think that this was what the voice had been saying to him about going home. This might be the solution to his uncertainty about what to do. He had loved the taste of construction work that he had back in Kathmandu. And based on how his parents' health seemed to be faltering, this seemed like it might be a way to pay them back for all they had done for him over the years.

They laid out all the details for Ram as to how he could join them; there was no shortage of jobs, they assured him. That he had some experience already would be a bonus and he could come live with them in the small house they had acquired. Ram suddenly felt elated and like he had found his direction.

It all sounded perfect – except for the fact that he had no money to get himself to Egypt. That would be necessary, and he no real money to speak of. All his support and living expenses back in Kathmandu were taken care of by the Kadys. His heart sank.

He did not, however, let this show. As usual, Ram was sure if this was his path, somehow, some way, it would all work out. In the meantime, he was in high spirits as he reconnected with his friends and looked forward to all that the festival would be offering.

The old friends talked and reminisced throughout the morning, until Ram realized how much time had elapsed. He reluctantly bid them farewell, promising to catch up to them again during the festival, and he hurried home to check on his parents.

On the way, the reality of what he wanted to do – to join his friends in Egypt – set in and Ram was overcome with a wave of despair, a rare occurrence for him. It was one thing to know in his heart that all would work out. It was another to make that plan become a reality.

Ram's parents were up and around as he arrived back at the house. He sat with them and shared their traditional breakfast of Masala Dosa and tea. The sun finally began to warm up the day and Ram went back outside with them to sit and visit.

Neighbors began to drop by to hear of how he was doing in Kathmandu. Ram smiled and passed along the same selected stories that he had shared with his parents. Everyone congratulated him on his fine English. It is a good day, Ram thought.

He let his worries about Egypt go for the moment, not wanting this to spoil his limited amount of time back in Chandisthan with his family. There would be time for worry later.

As his father sat and talked with one of his oldest friends in the village, Ram looked up toward Khudi Bazaar, trying to figure out when he might fit in a quick trip there. He always made at least one trek to the tourist mecca, just as a reminder of how much he loved interacting with all the American and European visitors.

Just as he was about to join his father and his friend, Ram caught some movement out of the corner of his vision, along the narrow but well-worn track that led from Chandisthan to Khudi Bazaar. It was not unheard of, but rare that anyone from the small village made their way down to Chandisthan.

And the gait of the person.... Ram knew from experience that it was not a Nepali. The way the person walked could only be that of a westerner – a seasoned hiker, to be sure, but definitely a tourist.

Ram continued to stare, wondering what would bring anyone from abroad down to them. Maybe they had heard of the local festival in Chandisthan and wanted to see how it differed from the one observed in Khudi Bazaar.

As time went by, Ram could see that the figure was a man. He was making good time, though, using a fancy, expandable walking stick to make his way along. Then, he just froze. It couldn't be...*but it was.*

Ram set his bowl from breakfast aside and moved to meet the man as he began to come into the village. It was his old friend from America, Mr. Garrison!

Mr. Garrison looked up as Ram approached him and smiled widely, waving. Ram could not believe his eyes. He ran closer, waving wildly.

"Mr. Garrison? What are you doing here?"

"Oh, I knew of the celebrations down here and I wanted to see them firsthand. I hoped you would be around, as well. Maybe it was time for me to come see you after all the times you made the trip to see me."

"I can't believe it! Please, come meet my family!"

Ram led his friend over to the house with great pride. Never would he have imagined that any of his acquaintances from Khudi Bazaar would come to see him! His father looked up, a puzzled look on his face, stopping in mid-conversation with his friend from the village.

"Mother! Come quickly! My friend from America, Mr. Garrison, has come to visit!"

Ram showed Mr. Garrison to a bench just outside the house, explaining in rapid Nepali to his parents who this was and that he had come down from Khudi Bazaar just to see them. Ram went back and forth between his parents and the other few neighbors who had begun to gather around during the commotion, translating between English and Nepali. Soon, there were broad smiles all around.

Ram's mother brought Mr. Garrison some food and tea. After all the excitement had passed, Ram sat with Garrison and talked at length, just as they always did up at Khudi Bazaar.

"So, Ram, you are still in Kathmandu? Going to school?"

Ram hesitated, then confided all that was on his mind to the man: his feeling that he had gotten all he could out of his schooling, his parents' faltering health, and how he had the opportunity to go with his friends to Egypt to make money that he could send home to support them. Garrison listened with all his attention, impressed at the young boy's dedication to his family and desire for more out of his life.

At this point, Ram had not imparted how he had no idea where he was going to get the funds to make this journey, only that this was his plan. Mr. Garrison, though, could see a look of concern on Ram's face even as he enthusiastically described his idea. He looked around at relatively meager surroundings of Chandisthan. It seemed an ambitious goal.

"So, Ram, tell me. When the festival is over, you will leave with your friends?"

"Well, sir-"

Mr. Garrison held up his hand and Ram stopped speaking.

"Please, call me Roger. We have known each other now for years."

"Yes...Roger."

"So, you are leaving with them?"

"I...uh...well...I am not sure."

"You sounded so sure when you were telling me about it."

"I can stay with them in Samalout. It's just that getting there that is a problem."

Ram had not intended to divulge any of this to Roger, but he seemed insistent on hearing the story. He went into some detail, letting Roger know that he had no real money to speak of with his role in Kathmandu. There had been a small initial payment to Ram's parents for the arrangement, but the Kadys were supporting him there and paying for his schooling in trade for his work as their house boy. He felt ashamed as he unburdened his soul to his friend and looked at his feet.

Roger just nodded and looked over at Ram, hesitating before he said anything further. He was somewhat familiar with the culture in Nepal, but made extra efforts not to do or say anything that might make him appear insensitive to them.

He had seen the frailty of Ram's parents, though, and was touched that the boy wanted to shoulder the burden of his family at such a young age. It was unfair. But maybe he could make it better. Roger sighed and plunged ahead, hoping he was not overstepping some hidden cultural standard.

"Ram?"

Ram looked up slowly, still feeling awkward for all that he had said.

"You are sure this is what you really want to do?"

"If I had the travel expenses…yes."

"What if I told you that it was taken care of? Would you still want to go?"

Ram looked at Roger, having no idea what he was talking about.

"Taken care of? I do not understand."

"Let me see if I can explain it better. Ram, I live in Oregon, back in America. Do you know where that is?"

Ram nodded. He had pored over maps of America ever since he had met Roger years ago, trying to get a better idea of what America was all about.

"Well, I had a son once. His name was Peter. I never thought I would have children, but when Peter was born, it changed my life completely. He was a gift, you know?" Roger paused, letting the quaver in his voice pass by. "Then, one day, with no warning, when Peter was about as young as you were when we first met...he got sick. Very sick. We had doctors from all over try and cure him, but no one could do anything. It was like a part of me died, too. Does that make sense?"

Ram nodded. His friend from childhood, Nigam, had died when they were just five. It had nearly destroyed Nigam's father.

"I finally got over it, but it took a long, long time. Then, one day, I came to Nepal to trek around the Annapurnas. It was one of my lifelong goals. I met you and it was like being around Peter again. You have a lot of the spirit and enthusiasm that my Peter had. You brought life back into my life."

Ram nodded as he listened, having no idea that adults ever spoke of these things in this way. It was foreign to him so far in his life.

"If you would let me...I would like to see that the lack of money does not prevent you from pursuing this dream." Ram felt his mouth drop open. He did not know what to say. "Have you talked about this idea with your parents?"

"Not yet. Until now, it just did not seem possible, so I just kept it to myself."

"Why don't we talk to them? If they approve, I'd like to help."

Ram sat still, stunned at what he was hearing. Sure, he always believed that if things were meant to be, they would happen. But this had come out of the blue and he was having a hard time believing it was real. At this point, he had no idea if his parents would even approve of his going so far away. But he sure wanted to do this, if possible.

He looked at Roger, smiled, and nodded. They entered the house and Ram translated between Roger and his parents as he explained the whole situation.

It took a bit of convincing to get his mother on board, but Ram and Roger finally got everyone to agree. Ram was still amazed. *The voice had said to go home.* From this message, he had found out about the opportunity with his friends. And now, through a relationship he had made years ago with this kind American, it was all coming to fruition.

Never again would he doubt the signs he received from his prayers and meditations. He had no idea how to thank his friend, Roger, or how he was ever to pay him back for his generosity.

"This is not a loan, Ram. It is a gift. Do not concern yourself any further. Just be the best you can be, no matter what it is you should do in your life, okay?"

"I will. There is just one other thing, though. The family I am working for in Kathmandu?"

"The Kadys, I believe?"

"Yes. They will be returning here for me in a week. I have no way of getting in touch with them to let them know I will not be returning."

"I see."

"But it's more than that, Roger. They have been very good to me. It was not so good in the beginning, but lately, it's been great. It's not that I cannot contact them myself, but I feel bad just taking off like this."

"Of course. They have a telephone there in the new house?"

"Yes."

"Give me their full name and the new address. I will take care of it and make sure they understand. I am sure they would want what is best, right?"

"I suppose. But I still feel guilty."

"That is human, Ram. You have more than fulfilled what they hired you for, I bet. I will handle it. You just take care."

"I do not know how to thank you, Roger. I just...." Ram's voice trailed off as he felt himself near tears.

"Trust me, Ram. You have thanked more over the years than you will ever know. This is my payment back. We are more than blessed in my country. It is just money. I will never miss it. Chances are we may never see each other again. I am getting a bit too old now for another trip back here, and I suspect you will go on to great things elsewhere."

Ram looked up to see a tear falling down Roger's cheek. He ran and hugged the man in response. Roger handed Ram a small burlap satchel, then picked up his walking stick and began the hike back up the hill to Khudi Bazaar as the sun set behind them.

He watched until Roger was out of view, then opened the satchel. It had more rupees inside than Ram had ever seen in one place in his life. At the bottom of the satchel was a small photo. It was of Roger and Ram when they had first met at Khudi Bazaar years before. Ram appreciated the money, but the photo meant even more.

His heart filled with warm feelings of thankfulness and a new level of closeness to Roger. He smiled, thinking there was no shortage of good people in this world.

14.

Egypt

The final day of the festival came sooner than Ram was expecting. He gathered what few possessions he had in preparation for the journey to Egypt with his friends. Ram was glad he had brought most of his personal possessions back to Chandisthan from Kathmandu, as this trip was very sudden. Most of all, he was glad he had packed the beloved dog-eared book he had gotten from Roger many years before.

Roger had left him more than what he would need to make the trip, so he handed over the surplus to his father in case they needed some extra to get them through the winter. He promised to write as often as he could, and that he would soon be sending money to them regularly.

He had heard of friends who had made similar promises but forgot about their parents as soon as they got to the foreign land. He took a moment to make a promise to himself that he would put his parents before himself and only spend for necessities. Taking care of his elderly parents was more important to him than anything he could buy for himself.

This goodbye was going to be tougher than last. He had been mentally preparing himself to be strong for everyone's sake and leave home smiling. He wanted them to remember him smiling. No matter how hard he tried, when the time came for him to leave, Ram felt a thick lump in his throat.

He had well expected an emotional farewell from his mother, but when he saw tears in his father's eyes, he started having serious doubts about leaving. He thought about cancelling the trip to stay close to everyone. He had never known his father to react in such a way, but he finally tore away from them and joined his friends as they prepared to make the long ride to Kathmandu, then the even longer trek to Egypt.

Ram had never been out of Nepal before; all he knew of the Middle East was what he had read in some history books in school. His friends had given him some highlights and some stories of what to expect, but they assured him that learning it first-hand was the best.

Ram pulled out the photo of Roger and himself often during the multi-day journey, offering up his gratitude and thanks daily over his fortune to have met such a wonderful man.

*****

The arrival in Egypt was yet another culture shock for Ram. As busy as Kathmandu had been, it was just a warm-up for what he encountered as he and his friends motored from Cairo to Samalout.

It was not just the hustle and bustle of the towns, either. At least in Kathmandu, Ram had been around people that he was familiar with: their looks, their dress, their food, and their customs. Here in Egypt, all of this was new, and as foreign to Ram as if he had landed on another planet.

And the weather! Ram was used to the heat of Kathmandu in the summer, but here in Egypt, it was early winter and it was still hotter than anything Ram had ever known in a Nepalese summer. *And so arid!*

He guessed he would get used to it, but as a first exposure, it was almost overwhelming. Ram realized, too, that there would be another language barrier. Though English was spoken widely and his friends assured him that on the job site, that would be sufficient, it was unnerving to be thrust into a place where rapidly-spoken Arabic was everywhere.

Ram accompanied his friends to the small house that the construction company provided for all the workers who were not Egyptian nationals. They showed him where he would be staying: a small but clean room he could share with the three of them. The house was filled with men from all over, who, like Ram, had arrived for the chance to make more money here than they could in their native homes.

Once they had stowed their things, they took Ram on a quick tour of the town so he could get his bearings. They also bought him some clothes that were more appropriate for the climate, both for working and otherwise. As a final trip, they ran him by the office of the construction company so Ram could introduce himself and make sure the owner knew he had construction experience, spoke good English, and was available to start right away.

The "interview" went well and the owner told Ram to report to him the next morning with his friends. He was short-handed and Ram had arrived at just the right moment. His previous experience and language skills put a smile on his face, as well. Ram was excited, nervous, and curious.

They all turned in early to make sure Ram made a good impression on his first day. The room he was sharing with his friends, Adarsh, Nirijan, and Sudi was a simple square, but it allowed each of them adequate space. After his boyhood home in Chandisthan, sharing first the small bedroom with Chandra and Manu, and then, his private space under the steps in Kathmandu, Ram felt this was elegant by comparison.

He had a comfortable sleeping pad, plus a small set of shelves where he stored the book that Roger had given him long ago. He folded his few clothes in neat piles under the shelves. The only other real possession that Ram owned was the photo he had just acquired of himself with Roger at Khudi Bazaar, when he was maybe eleven or twelve. Ram made sure he looked at it each morning and evening to make sure he never forgot the kindness he had been the recipient of. He placed the photo well inside the pages of the book to keep it clean and undamaged, fearing the climate of Samalout might take its toll on it.

As always, Ram began and ended his day with meditation. Adarsh, Nirijan, and Sudi sometimes joined him in his practices, but they often became distracted or neglectful toward this. Ram found himself a solo participant, as he had in Kathmandu.

No matter what had happened during his day, good or bad, Ram always made the time. It had been so instrumental in the direction his life had taken thus far that Ram could not imagine letting it lapse. Even in the darkest times of his early days in Kathmandu, Ram had been comforted and supported by his prayers of gratitude and thankfulness, no matter how small the gift might have seemed at the time.

He wondered from time to time what the Kadys' reaction had been to his sudden and unannounced departure. Ram still felt a bit guilty about this, but in the end, he knew that his priority now was to take care of his parents. He did not spend an inordinate amount of time fretting over it. They were a wealthy family and he was sure they could easily replace him.

He did miss the comradery with Chandra and Manu, though. The three of them had made such strides together as their friendship had grown, and he would miss that dearly. He thought of them as his own siblings. After all, he had spent more time with them than his own siblings. Ram wanted to let the Kadys know it was not anything that they did, which let to this decision. He guessed they would be taken aback when Roger contacted them, but at least he had saved them a wasted trip to and from Kathmandu. Ram would have wanted to say goodbye to the Kadys in person but may be one less goodbye was not a bad thing for him after all.

Roger was a gentle and friendly man. He was sure that even if the Kadys were angry or otherwise put out over his decision, Roger had been able to smooth things over and explain the situation completely. It was the not knowing that was nagging at Ram. That, plus the very real possibility that he might never see Roger again.

Like a lot of nights for Ram when he began a new chapter in his life, he fell asleep with a storm of thoughts and emotions swirling in his mind. Unlike Kathmandu, though, Ram slept peacefully this first night. He dreamt, but the images were pleasant and serene.

*****

The heat of the morning woke Ram. He wondered how long it would take to adjust to it. The streets outside were already alive with people busy with their day: merchants setting up their wares, children running about playing and on their way to school, women sweeping and cleaning their doorways, plus many more that Ram had yet come to understand.

Spiritual influence was part of this, as well. The sounds and behaviors associated with the area were intriguing to Ram as he watched from the small balcony of their room. He had no idea what the Arabic meant that wafted across the air from surrounding mosques and temples, but it was pleasant to his ear. He smiled, assuming it was just another version of what he practiced.

Adarsh, Nirijan, and Sudi arose just as Ram was completing his own prayers. The four of them washed quickly in the shared bath in the hallway. Then, they stopped at a small stand just around the corner for tea, fuul, and ta'amiya. Ram looked suspiciously at the array of offerings. Both were utterly foreign to him, but Nirijan assured him they were both wonderful.

"What exactly are those?" Ram asked.

"Fuul is the traditional local breakfast," Sudi answered. "It is an acquired taste, but you will appreciate it greatly once we get to work. It will be a long time until we get lunch break. They bake the pita bread in the stone ovens, then stuff them with mashed fava beans."

"And those?" Ram pointed to the oddly colored patties that lay on a platter nearby.

"Ah," replied Nirijan, "ta'amiya is my favorite. Do you know of falafel?" Ram nodded. This had been a popular dish in Pokhara that he had tried once or twice with his father. "They're much like falafel, but they are much moister. The locals make them with fava beans instead of garbanzo beans. They're very nice."

Ram shrugged, trusting his friends. He joined them as they sat on a low wall and ate. He winced a bit as he bit into the fuul, understanding what Sudi had meant about an acquired taste. Not only were the beans cold, but they were a bit bitter. It was only the wonderful texture and flavor of the fresh pita that made Ram appreciate the dish.

The ta'amiya, on the other hand, he found delicious. The tahini sauce that came with them made the small patties utterly delectable to Ram's palate. He had to agree that this version was a vast improvement over those he had tried back in Nepal.

As they ate, Ram got a quick overview of what they would be working on, as well as some cautions on working as a Nepali migrant. The buildings themselves, he found out, would be very similar to what Ram had experienced in Kathmandu: sand and bricks. He felt good about this, knowing that at least on a basic level, he would have some background as he began.

"If you just follow directions, do not complain, and make sure you are always busy, you will be fine."

"Be sure to never complain about anything", they reiterated.

Ram nodded. After all the bumps in the road he had gone through in his early days with the Kadys, he knew how to do this. The new place, new people, new food did not scare him as much. He was still a teenager, but life had put him through enough to give the wisdom of a grown man. He felt like he could take on any challenge and feeling of excitement was clearly visible on his face. This part, he was thankful for.

"The bosses are not unreasonable or mean, but they do expect a full day's work from us. In general, a lot of our fellow Nepalis and workers from other countries can get taken advantage of. But this company? So far, they have been good to work for. The work is hard, but the pay is good."

"Others get taken advantage of?"

Adarsh looked to the others for unspoken permission to explain. They just shrugged, indicating to go ahead.

"There is a system of sponsorship in Egypt called kefala. It's probably in other places in the Middle East, as well. For us to work here, a sponsor is required, but how the sponsorship works varies from company to company. We know a couple guys from India who work under a much different system than we do."

"Oh?"

"The company we work for? They have the same sponsorship as everyone else—it is required—but we have a lot more freedom. Under the typical kefala, foreign migrant workers can be under a contract whereby they are required to remain here for two years. They cannot leave for any circumstance unless they get permission from their sponsor."

"Even if there was a family emergency, or a funeral?"

"That is how the typical system works. The sponsor keeps your passport and other documents and will only return it back to the worker after the contract period is over"

"But not with our boss?"

"No. The owner of the construction company got his start abroad and apparently, he was subjected to a similar type of servitude. It rubbed him the wrong way, so he adheres to the registration with the Egyptian government since it is a law, but otherwise, we can come and go much more freely than some others. All he ever asks is some lead time if you need to go back to Nepal for something."

"What about an emergency?" Ram was thinking about his parents' health.

"He will work with you, if necessary. Just go and talk to him."

"Seems nice."

"So far, we have no complaints. He pays well, helped us get settled in the house we share, and he has never made unreasonable demands of us on the job site. And the best part? We have always gotten annual leave for the festival back in Chandisthan."

Ram smiled as they approached the house that was under construction. It was abuzz with activity and they waved to the other workers as they came closer. Ram left his friends to check in with the owner, feeling like he had stumbled into a wonderful situation.

He took the seat offered by the large man as he explained how they worked on the site and what he wanted Ram to do. A lot of what he told Ram reaffirmed what he had heard from his friends. He signed some paperwork, shook the man's hand, and set off across the yard to begin his new job.

15.

Priya

The work was similar to what Ram had experienced in Kathmandu. He began the day hauling bricks and sand, much as he had when he had helped the workers with the Kadys' new home. It was hard, but since Ram already had a taste of this kind of routine, he found it easier than he might have if he had no experience.

The thing that was challenging him was the heat. It was almost unbearable, causing rivulets of sweat to pour down his body. One of the workers gave him some hints on how to cope with that and Ram plugged along, making the best of it. Sudi had been right, though; the hearty breakfast had been crucial. By mid-day, when they got a break, Ram was whipped.

He watched everyone around him and saw what they did to regenerate for the afternoon and just copied what he saw. By the end of the day, Ram seemed to have melded in well with the construction team. Many that were strangers that morning were treating him like a good friend by the end of the day. Certainly, his work ethic was a big part of it, but when they saw that he had hands-on experience from Kathmandu, he was soon upgraded from an errand boy to one of them.

Ram was moving much more slowly on the way home with Adarsh, Nirijan, and Sudi than he had that morning, but the day had been a good one. He was tired, but it was a good kind of tired.

Ram was sure each day would be more adaptable for him weather-wise and he was getting the same satisfaction from what he was doing here as he had in Kathmandu. Psychologically, Ram loved the idea of making something, to be able to look one day and know he was a part of some new structure.

As he had thought, it was just a matter of time for him to adjust to the heat. He soon made a reputation as a hard-working, capable, and honest part of the team. There was great comradery among the workers.

Ram got something else out of the job, though, that he had not anticipated: he was learning about other countries and cultures. The team was split among Egyptian locals and other migrants from all over. During breaks and as they worked, Ram talked to his fellow workers to hear of how they had come to be here. He also got a first-hand, practical life lesson on what it was like to have grown up in Egypt. None of them knew each other's language. However, between few English words, Arabic words, and some gesturing they had no difficulty communicating with each other.

The culture of Egypt was so different than anything Ram had ever been exposed to; he listened with fascination. This was what he was missing, he felt, from just sitting all day in a classroom in Kathmandu: real life experience and real word learning.

In just a few short weeks, Ram felt like he had learned more things that he could use in his life than in all the time he sat in class. It was wonderful. He finally felt like the characters in the TV. He still did not have fancy clothes to wear or delicacies to eat like the people on TV. He was however, seeing new places and learning new things and that was enough.

He met men from various countries in Africa who had come here for the same reasons as Ram had. There was little opportunity for them at home and they needed a better way to support their families. They came from places that Ram had never heard of, such as Libya, Chad, and Sudan. Men came from other parts of the Middle East, as well, and even as far away as Turkey, Pakistan, and India. It was an interesting mix of people, but other than the occasional disagreement, everyone seemed to work together well.

Of all the men Ram met, he made the closest friendship with a man not much older than himself, named Mereruka. His family was originally from Lebanon, but as the ongoing conflicts there had grown and grown, Mereruka moved to Egypt with his parents and sister when he was just five. His father had been a successful importer with a shop right on the Mediterranean Sea.

Ram didn't know much about the ocean, except what he had read about in *The Old Man and the Sea*, and he became enthralled with the stories of Mereruka's childhood home. It was a place called Byblos, located between Beirut and Tripoli. The descriptions of the blue water lapping at the shores and hundreds of boats anchored in the cove lit up Ram's imagination.

Despite having been forced to flee from Byblos due to numerous conflicts that spilled over from Beirut, Mereruka seemed to have a deep love and fond memories of the town. His father lost most of the wealth that he had amassed in Lebanon when they relocated, but in retrospect, the timing was perfect.

Mereruka had heard hideous stories of what had happened to their neighbors that stayed behind, hoping the wars would just peter out. There was a real look of pain in his face, and his eyes took on a distant, haunted look as he shared this with Ram.

Ram did not push any further with this. He had no idea what might have really happened, but it was obvious that Mereruka was troubled by just the memory. Just the fact that his new friend had been comfortable enough to share such an ordeal with him was enough.

It was the first time that Ram had ever met someone that had experienced such a traumatic life and he was shocked. They had struggled financially ever since arriving in Egypt and he was now trying to help his family, much like Ram was with his folks.

As foreign as the sea was to Ram, the towering peaks of the Himalayas were just as foreign to Mereruka. He sat wide-eyed as Ram shared his stories of growing up in the shadow of the Annapurnas; of the drastic changes in seasons; his excursions to Pokhara with his father; his fortuitous friendship with the American hiker, Roger Garrison, who had been his benefactor to allow him to come to Egypt; and finally, his experience in Kathmandu with the Kadys.

It certainly was not the ordeal that Mereruka had gone through with his family, but it was all that Ram had to offer. He even relayed his sad tale of unrequited love for the neighbor girl and Mereruka joined Ram in laughter when he finished the story.

Ram and Mereruka took to spending their lunch break together. Ram, with his friend's help, began to learn some Arabic – at least some key phrases so he could communicate with the food vendors and other merchants in town more easily. Mereruka was Muslim and he helped Ram understand a lot of the spiritual practices he was seeing in town. In return, Ram gave him the highlights of his Buddhist upbringing. Lo and behold, as Ram had suspected, the two faiths had a lot in common.

Picking up some Arabic helped Ram all over town; he soon found more and more friends, once the language barrier came down a bit. Other than Mereruka, Ram tended to socialize with just Adarsh, Nirijan, and Sudi, as a lot of the workers he knew were much older and many had families to attend to once work was over. The four Nepali friends and Mereruka soon became fast friends and it was unusual to ever see them around Samalout not in the company of one another.

Ram was amazed once he started getting paid, as well. It certainly seemed to be everything that he had been told back in Chandisthan. He could live well and set aside a large proportion for his family, as had been predicted. He could finally take good care of Ama and Baba like he had promised them. He thought of how amazing it would be to take Baba to Pokhara and be able to buy lassis for both of them. The thought of spending an evening by the lake, drinking lassis with Baba lightened up his face. Tears started rolling down his cheeks, but these were tears of joy. Ram's hard work and determination was finally paying dividends.

Each year, as the fall festival came around, Ram headed home with Adarsh, Nirijan, and Sudi. He was thrilled to be able to hand over enough money to fully get his parents through the winter. In good years, his father had some repairs and alterations made to the house that had been neglected for some time. Also, they were able to get better medical attention that often had to be put off due to other, more pressing concerns. In bad years, the money was there to make sure they did not have to scrimp on food or other necessities in the long, cold months until spring arrived.

A few years went by and this routine was what Ram's life consisted of. He was still learning more and more of the construction processes. The foreman gave him additional responsibilities based on his hard work, honesty, and language skills.

Ram was content with all of this until, one day, he saw a young Egyptian girl in town that reminded him of the neighbor girl in Kathmandu. Ram always smiled and waved when she did, but for obvious reasons, he was still a bit shy when it came to girls.

However, the idea of having this in his life began to occur to him more and more. It was on his latest trip home, when he was handing out the gifts that he brought back from Egypt, that this subject was raised by his mother. She inquired slyly about his intentions for a wife and Ram blushed.

He knew that by his village's standards, he was well past the point in time when he would have taken a wife and started his own family. It had occurred to him on a regular basis now, though he was shy and still stinging from the memory of his previous attempt at love.

Ama just nodded and smiled in her own curious way. She knew of a girl over in Baglungpani that she thought would be perfect. This neighboring village was just west of Chandisthan, and her family was similar to theirs, both economically and spiritually. Most importantly, they were from the same caste.

Intercaste marriages were starting to become common in the cities, but in village like Ram's, it was still rare. Mr. and Mrs. Kady were the only ones with an intercaste marriage that Ram knew of. Even that was between the top two castes. Once Ram returned to Egypt after the festival, Ama decided that it was time to make a visit to the family and possibly arrange a marriage between Ram and the daughter, Priya.

*****

Ama did not know the family well, so she spent some time visiting them. She invited them to Chandisthan so that both families could become better acquainted and make sure the union of their families was acceptable to all.

Priya was young, just sixteen, but by local mores, at prime age for marriage. She was small and thin, her body toned from the years of working on her family's farm. She was darker-skinned than Ram, with just a touch of Tibetan features in her face. Her dark hair, which she normally kept tied back, allowed her pretty facial features to radiate.

Ama was sure Ram would approve, but she had to move fast. She was sure that a girl as young and beautiful as Priya would soon be highly sought after by other families close by. All the various meetings of the two families went well, and a firm verbal contract was agreed to by all.

They would proceed with the marriage the following spring or summer. Everyone preferred spring. A wedding during the monsoon would not be ideal. It all depended on when Ram could get enough time off from work to come home.

*****

Ram arrived home one day to find a parcel addressed to him. It had obviously been in transit for some time. The return address was not indicated, so he had no idea who this might be from or what it was about, but the postage indicated it had come from Kathmandu via Pokhara.

At first, he was alarmed that it might be something bad from the Kadys, but the passage through Pokhara erased that thought. Then, he became even more alarmed that, perhaps, it was bad news from Chandisthan. He felt his skin run cold and his mouth dry up even more than it normally did here.

He slowly and hesitantly slit open the large envelope, praying it was something else. Ram inverted the open envelope and a single sheet of paper fell out, along with the photo of a young girl.

The photo slid under his shelves and he retrieved it. He sat down to read the letter, still confused and concerned. Ram just glanced at the photo as he set it aside, noticing only how attractive her face was.

He immediately recognized the handwriting as that of one of the neighbors in Chandisthan, though the wording and message was obviously from his mother. He read quickly to get the main points of the letter and breathed a deep sigh of relief when his initial scan of it did not reveal any type of emergency. Ram sat back against the warm wall of the room and read the letter again with more care, referring to the photo as he went.

He read it twice more, smiling widely each time. His parents had found a girl back home for him to marry and his mother had included all the details of what would proceed. Ram picked up the photo again and was stunned at the smiling beauty that looked back at him. He had never visited Baglungpani, knowing only that it was close by Chandisthan with a similar population and economy. He set the photo on the shelving so that it had a prominent display. He could hardly wait to tell Mereruka and his friends from home.

They were as excited and happy for Ram as he was once they found out, taking him out immediately to celebrate. Ram had always known this day would come, but now that things were in motion, it seemed unreal, like he was observing it happen to someone else. Ram sent a letter back home, telling everyone how wonderful this was and how excited he was, voicing his approval of the union.

After making some special arrangements, through extra work between now and the marriage, Ram's boss had agreed for him to take two weeks off for the ceremony in the late spring.

*****

Ram continued with his normal routine, including some extra work for his boss, and before he knew it, he was en route back to Nepal for his wedding. He was both excited and nervous as he travelled, wondering how he and his new wife would take to each other.

Even after he arrived back in Chandisthan, he knew that, by tradition, he would not meet Priya until the day of the wedding. There were a lot of pre-wedding activities, as many of Ram's relatives flowed into the village to take part in the celebration. The pre-wedding festivities went on for days, as gifts were exchanged and blessings were bestowed by various priests.

On the wedding day, Ram arose early to perform his personal meditation to calm his racing mind. He dressed in a more formal set of clothes than he ever had before, though not the ornately stunning garb that would normally be seen on the bride and groom. That is not to say they were simple, though. The wedding attire was colorful and distinctive, just not to the degree that some weddings in larger towns might observe. Chandisthan and Baglungpani were both small and relatively simple and reserved places, both in appearance and population. To agree with that natural façade, the clothes that Ram dressed in were likewise subtler and more reserved.

Over in Baglungpani, the bride's family and close friends observed the traditional day of fasting and performed ceremonies where they honored and worshipped their own ancestors. Meanwhile, in Chandisthan, the Janti kicked off in full swing. The Janti is often compared to the Baraat, the traditional Indian version, with a loud and cheerful gathering of all the people associated with the groom. Ram was then loaded onto the most ornate and decorated horse-drawn cart that was in Chandisthan for the trip to Baglungpani.

Ram and his relatives and friends arrived at Priya's home and her family walked around him three times, throwing blessed rice and flower petals over everyone. Ram was then moved to a pida, a wooden seat in the center of the main courtyard of the village. Priya's father appeared from their home, where he formally greeted Ram and offered the traditional pre-ceremony food to Ram and his guests. After a few minutes, Ram was instructed to move to another part of the courtyard for the actual ceremony, beginning with the Kanyadaan.

Ram was seated, facing East, in the mandap – the wedding stage where the vows were to be exchanged. He waited, his heart pounding, as Priya approached. He looked up as she took her own spot opposite of him and they looked upon one another for the very first time.

Ram felt himself short of breath as he gazed on Priya in all her fine wedding regale. The photo had not done her justice. As he smiled at her, Priya averted her eyes, blushing. To an outsider, this might have seemed odd, but it was a very traditional show of approval and respect. Ram, however, did not miss her equally pleasing smile toward him just before she looked away.

The priest performing the Kanyadaan then spread a yellow cloth over them and stepped aside. Priya's father completed the formal giving away of the bride with a kalash of water, mango leaves, fig leaves, camphor, betel nuts, and grass, the entire vessel tied with sacred thread. The vessel represented abundance and the source of life and was left as he stood away.

This was followed by the godadhuwa, in which both Ram's and Priya's feet were washed by the Priya's relatives. Ram was then handed a conch shell filled with grass, rice, yogurt, fruit and sandalwood mixed into water, which was sprinkled on his head. Afterward, he was fed a mix of ghee, yogurt, and honey.

Ram and Priya were then led inside a home to a room known as the guptaghar, where Ram offered new clothes to Priya. Simultaneously, Ram was given new clothes by Priya's family, which he changed into. Between the two sets of new garments was a short length of cloth, trying the clothes together and representing the linkage of Ram and Priya together.

Priya's father placed Ram's right hand over Priya's and announced that he was giving her away, then asked Ram to accept her. The priest then completed a series of prayers and placed small red marks, known as tika, on both Ram and Priya. Ram clasped Priya's thumb and began the vows.

"You are the Earth and I the sky. Please let us marry and have children. May they be strong and successful. May we live for a hundred years in good health."

Priya took a step and leaned on Ram's shoulder for support as Ram uttered his own prayers. They concluded by offering popped rice to a small fire as they circled the flames three times. Ram offered Priya a colorful necklace locally known as pote, glass bead necklaces indicating marriage, one each of red, yellow, and green.

Then, he applied sindhoor, the traditional vermillion red powder, to the part in her hair. This was well-known as an indication that the woman is married when she is in public. Ram applied the sindhoor a total of three times. Upon the third application, they were then considered officially married.

Priya and Ram then exchanged necklaces made of grass, followed by wedding rings. Priya bowed to Ram, placing her forehead on the tops of his feet, after which she prepared ghee, honey and yogurt in a bowl, mixing it with her index finger. She then offered half to Ram, finishing the other half herself.

It was an all-day event, but rather than being exhausted, both Ram and Priya looked and felt exhilarated and radiant. Priya joined Ram in the horse-drawn cart that had brought him to Baglungpani and they made the short but very bumpy ride back to Chandisthan.

Priya felt a thickness in her throat as she said her farewells to her family and her village, but she also felt wildly optimistic as she embarked on her new life with Ram.

16.

The Tapestry

Ram and Priya set themselves up in the small addition that Ram and his father had made to their original house. It did not offer a lot of privacy, but was a vast improvement, Ram thought, on having to add yet another person to the already well-occupied main house.

The first night, they just sat up late into the night, talking and exchanging stories. They realized they knew little of each other's lives prior to the wedding. Priya sat in amazement as she took in all the paths that had led Ram to this day, from his friendship with Roger Garrison to his service and schooling in Kathmandu to his new job now in Samalout.

Ram was hesitant to share his misadventure in love from Kathmandu, but Priya was now his wife, so he wanted to share everything with her. Her mouth went to a shocked "O" as he retold the tale of his flogging at the hands of the girl's mother and subsequent rescue by Mr. Kady. He could not stop himself from laughing as he thought back on the incident and how naïve he had been. By the time he finished the story, she joined him in laughter.

It was late into the night, or very early into the next morning, when Ram and Priya finally ran out of energy and fell asleep together as man and wife.

Neither Ram nor Priya had any experience in an intimate relationship; at first, they were both awkward and clueless. However, as the days and nights went on, this all became more natural for both of them and together, they learned.

Ram had just a limited time here before he had to get back to Samalout and his job, so they made the most of their time together as possible. Their days were spent travelling around to all the relatives and friends who had not been able to make it to the wedding ceremony. Ram was proud as he met with everyone showing off his new wife. He could not remember a time in his life when he had been happier.

With his new flow of income, Ram even took Priya over to Pokhara to show her around the place that had been such a special treat for him when he was a child. She had never been much beyond Baglungpani, so the size and activity of Pokhara was thrilling. They took a long walk down to Phewa Lake and sat under the shade of the large leafy trees that hung over the banks. They relaxed and watched the men go out to fish the depths of the lake for the delicacies that would soon be served to the tourists.

Priya, like Ram, was utterly content with her new life as his wife and she felt blessed to have him in her life. Time passed and they arose from their lounging lakeside to wander the peaceful and scenic lane that ran by the lake.

Priya was looking longingly in some of the shops offering handmade tapestries, scarfs, and other niceties. Ram saw this and told her to pick something out that she loved more than anything. She was sure he was just trying to show an interest in what she was looking over. She stopped at a tapestry that was in a shop just beyond the stall where he and his father had bought lassis to celebrate their trips here.

"You like it?"

"Oh, yes. It's so lovely."

Ram walked over to the owner; Priya stood back, watching the conversation. After a few moments of negotiation, she saw Ram hand the man some rupees. He removed the tapestry from its hanger and carefully wrapped it up in some brown parchment. Ram shook his hand and accepted the package, then returned to where Priya was standing.

He smiled, looked into her large brown eyes, and handed the package to her.

"A gift for you, to remind you of our time together when I am away in Egypt."

Priya was stunned. She had never, in her wildest imagination, thought that something so beautiful and fine would be hers. *And to have the money to purchase such a thing!* It was beyond her comprehension. She held the parcel, not knowing what to say.

"Really? Are you sure? It is so expensive!"

"I am. It is nothing."

Priya felt her eyes fill with tears of appreciation and love from this simple yet generous kindness from her new husband. She tucked the light parcel under her arm and took Ram's arm with her free hand. They continued their stroll along the street back toward the lake.

Just as they were about to reach the cart and ox that they had used to travel here, Ram stopped and looked closely at one of the cafés. He thought back to all the trips he had made here with his father and how he had longed to be able to partake in a meal, like one of the tourists from the West.

"Are you hungry, Priya?"

"A bit. Why?"

"Would you like to have something to eat here before we return?"

"Could we?"

Ram held out his hand, indicating for her to go over to one of the tables that sat outside the café. He held her chair for her and then took his own seat near her. They had a small and simple lunch, but to Ram, it was the fulfillment of a dream he had harbored for many years.

As he tasted the delicate pieces of golden mahseer, local fish brought fresh from Phewa Lake, he could not believe his good fortune. Here he was, a simple man from a remote village, eating like a visitor with his beautiful new wife. It made him nearly burst with gratitude and appreciation.

*****

Priya was even more overwhelmed with the experience. She had never been to such a large town before, and now to have the trip topped off with an elegant gift and a magnificent meal! She felt like a princess in one of the stories her mother had told her as a young girl.

She was still reeling at her fortune to have Ram as her husband; he was so thoughtful and loving. They lingered over the last bits of the lunch before Ram suggested they begin the long ride home so that they would get back before they lost the sun completely.

They rode the well-worn, uneven road back to Chandisthan, recounting their wonderful day in Pokhara. Priya held the parcel containing her new tapestry tight to her chest when they hit some of the more challenging bumps along the way, making sure this gift was extra safe. The sun began to fall quickly as they neared the village, but with Ram's expertise at driving the ox, they arrived just before the sun set behind the mountains.

He unleashed the ox and stored the cart away after taking care to feed the gentle beast. Priya went ahead to the house to show off her new tapestry to Ram's parents and to tell them of their day.

*****

Ram returned to the house, still feeling ecstatic over his new life and looking forward to many years of contentment and joy with Priya and the family they would someday create.

They sat with his parents and savored the meal his mother had prepared as he accepted all the accolades from his mother at his generosity and thoughtfulness for Priya. Ram just smiled and blushed a bit, as he was not used to such praise.

As the meal was ending, Ram excused himself and went outside. This was highly unusual in the household, and his mother and father looked on with curiosity. Priya just indicated she had no idea what he was up to.

They moved to the living area and Ram's father lit a small fire, as the temperature of the approaching night began to fall. As they talked, Ram soon reappeared with a satchel and sat with Priya. He reached into the bag and handed a box to his mother, then another to his father. They both looked on with furrowed brows, not understanding.

"Open them."

Ram leaned back and watched as his mother carefully undid the twine that was securing the lid and finally lifted the flap. She reached in and removed a medium-sized box decorated with elephants and embossed in gold and red embroidery. It was the same series of boxes that Ram had seen Mr. Kady bring home to his wife when he had returned from his business trip in India. She stared in disbelief as she removed each successively smaller box and arrayed them side by side.

His father beamed as he watched, and Ram indicated that he should open his, too. The package that Ram had handed him was long and narrow, as opposed to the nearly square one he had presented his mother with. He undid the thick string that held it together, then unfurled the brown wrapping paper that surrounded a new, handmade walking stick. It was made of a hardwood local to Pokhara and had intricate carvings along its length. There were some figures of animals and some small words in Nepalese for good fortune and a long, healthy life.

Priya now beamed at her husband as his parents stared back in incredulity. He had never seen his father cry, but there was no mistaking the high emotion in his father's face as he held his new walking stick out in appreciation.

"Ram," his mother finally said, wiping away a tear, "this is too much. You shouldn't have."

"Nonsense, mother. It is so little compared to everything I have received. I have so much now that I just want to share it with my family."

She nodded and smiled as she ran her fingers along the edges of the boxes, admiring them lovingly. Ram's father likewise ran his weathered fingers along the carvings of the stick as he read the inscribed words, each one being spoken with reverence and serious impart. The four of them talked a bit more, until Ram could see that his parents were tired. He said good night and he and Priya took their leave to their own space in the addition.

"When did you get all the gifts for your parents?"

"When I went up to talk to the owner of that shop where we bought your tapestry, I saw them off to the side while you were looking over all the cloths. I had them wrap them up at the same and take them to the cart. They knew me from all the trips here with my father over the years."

"That was very thoughtful."

"Once, when I was in Kathmandu, working for the Kadys? Mr. Kady came back from a business trip to India. He brought back gifts for his family. I had a warmer relationship with them by that point, but he did not bring anything back for me. I know I was not a member of the family, but seeing that stung. Mrs. Kady tried to make it up by having him give me something, but I knew it was not from India, but from their house. I always remembered how much that hurt and I never want anyone to feel left out."

Priya smiled at him as they lay down to sleep, filled with admiration and respect for this man that was now her husband. They talked a while longer as the wind picked up and rattled the roof and sides of the addition where they were staying. Ram knew it would hold, though. The only thing that he had a skill for now was construction, and he had been instrumental in the addition being built.

Priya snuggled in closer and they soon fell asleep, both dreaming of the road ahead.

17.

Departure

The remainder of Ram's time off for his wedding finally ended and he found himself very sad at the thought of departing. The couple of weeks he and Priya had spent together had been almost magical, and it had felt more like they had known each other for a lifetime.

On prior trips back, Ram had usually felt a pull to get back to Samalout and his friends and the work. To some degree, that was still there, but now, leaving behind his wife made it bittersweet. He knew he wanted to return to work to make sure he was providing adequate support for both his parents and Priya, but leaving was going to be extra hard this time.

He strapped down the last of his bags before heading back to the house with a heavy heart to say his farewell to everyone. He knew that Priya would be safe and taken care of with his parents, but all the same, it was very difficult to leave. He kissed Priya goodbye, hugged his parents, and made his way toward the long trek back to Egypt.

He held tightly onto the pote necklace from the wedding that Priya had given him to remember her by. He knew that each time he looked at it, the necklace would remind him of Priya and what he needed to do to insure their happiness. Ram fell asleep along the way, a lump in his throat, but with his eyes on the future.

*****

Ram arrived back in Samalout tired from the journey, but soon enlivened by the greetings of Mereruka, Adarsh, Nirijan, and Sudi. They nearly suffocated him with congratulations and bombarded him with a million questions about the wedding and Priya. It was nice.

Ram was still brimming with pride and joy over his marriage and it was warming to have close friends to share it all with. Mereruka was looking forward to his own wedding that was planned for the next year, and he was particularly interested in how Ram felt now that he was a husband. They all talked long into the night, wondering when they might be getting married, as well. The new aura around Ram seemed to suit him well. They were jealous of his seemingly indestructible new happiness.

Work began again the next day and Ram was thrust back into his old routine without another thought. He found himself pushing harder and offering more to his employer, partly to thank the man for his generosity in letting him go home for the wedding, and partly to move ahead in the company to continue making a better life for his family.

In an unexpected turn of events, Adarsh had to return home when word of his father's sudden death reached them. It was a sad day for the four friends. No one knew exactly what to say when they found out and Adarsh was gone from their midst, just like that.

It was not how Ram would have planned it out, but Adarsh's departure ended up being fortuitous to him. His boss stepped in and promoted Ram to the higher position that Adarsh had occupied, based on all his hard work and skill. It was more money, more responsibility, and fit Ram well. He was sad to know Adarsh was suffering this blow and he often prayed for his family, but he also was ready to accept the new opportunity that came with his departure.

Soon after, Nirijan injured his leg when a lift of bricks gave way and fell on him. It was not a serious injury, but he could no longer do his job and he, too, had to return to Chandisthan. It was a hard double-punch to Ram, but he carried on, keeping his family's well-being his main priority.

Work went on, picking up in intensity. The company was developing a reputation for being among the top organizations around that could not only meet all the deadlines that were expected of them, but also almost always coming in under budget. Word soon spread, and demand for them went up significantly.

Sudi, unfortunately, had departed from the company to join another firm in Cairo. Ram never quite got the real story, but what he was told was that Sudi had had a heated argument with one of the foremen that had been hired recently. The man went to the owner and filed a grievance, stating that Sudi was a lazy layabout and needed to be replaced.

Ram was sure this was not the case, as Ram knew Sudi to be as hard-working as anyone. Certainly, it had been something else, but Sudi had departed so quickly that Ram never got the chance to get the real story from him. They had not been as close friends as Ram and Adarsh were, but it was still odd to not be able to at least wish him well.

On top of that, the new foreman was peculiar. He was not well-liked among the workers, often berating and yelling at them to get things done. He worked them hard under the grueling Egyptian sun, sometimes even denying them water or rest until they had finished their shifts. It was so unlike the normal way they did things. It was strange that the man had been hired in the first place. He was so unlike the owner, whom Ram admired immensely.

He supposed he could have gone to the boss with his concerns and stood up for Sudi, but the departure was sudden and over and done with, as far as Ram knew. Also, and he supposed that it was a bit selfish and self-serving, but Ram wanted to protect his position and his family's future. He was well-liked and respected by his co-workers, as well as the owner.

But another voice inside him reminded him that he was just a foreign migrant worker; he did not want to risk disrupting the good arrangement he had established and possibly be dismissed himself. This left just Ram and Mereruka as the remaining pair of friends from their little group. It was different, but Ram and Mereruka had become such close friends that it was fine.

The pace of the projects picked up each month, and Ram found himself being asked to take on more and more new tasks. It was a frantic pace, but he was learning more and more about the overall process and felt as if he had finally found his calling in life. *It could not be more perfect*, Ram thought to himself, *unless it was back in Nepal.*

But for now, it was what it was and he worked hard, as he always had. The summer bled into the fall, and the festival in Chandisthan was just around the corner. Ram was looking forward to seeing Priya again, but he was a bit on edge about asking for the time away so soon after his last trip.

The good thing was that hardly a day went by that the owner did not compliment and express his appreciation to Ram for all that he was doing. On top of that, they had pushed through hard since the summer, and had finished up a set of apartments in record time, which resulted in a huge bonus for the company. The owner had spread this around and let everyone know that he was amazed by their skill and efficiency. He seemed in such good spirits that Ram figured this was his best chance to make the request.

He gathered all his courage and stopped by the main office as they were finishing up a small house for a long-time client. The owner waved him in enthusiastically and Ram took the seat that was offered.

He humbly presented his request, acknowledging that he had just been away recently. There it was. It was out. Ram figured the worst thing that could happen would be that his request would be denied. The look on the man's face as Ram made his proposal was neutral, giving Ram no idea where he stood.

"Ah, yes. The annual harvest festival," the owner said as he leaned back and interlocked his fingers behind his head.

"Yes, sir."

"Ram, I cannot tell you how impressed and pleased I have been with your work. You never complain, you are always looking for things that need to be done, even if you are not asked to handle them, and I have never had a worker here more honest and trustworthy."

"Thank you, sir. You are most kind."

"I know you are concerned about asking for this time away after your wedding. But right now, we are heading into a lull until next month and I see no reason that you should not go. I know you are missing your new wife and family. You have worked harder than anyone, so sure, no problem."

Ram could not believe his ears. It was like a weight had been lifted from his shoulders.

"Oh, thank you, sir. I cannot tell you how much this means to me."

"You are very welcome. This does come with one extra request, though."

"Of course, sir. Whatever you need."

"If I agree to let you go home for the festival, it would be so only if you agree to take over as the new field foreman upon your return."

Ram was stunned. Was he serious? He was not sure, but he did know that the current field foreman was unliked – and the man that had been responsible for Sudi's dismissal. It made no sense that he would be chosen, though.

"New field foreman, sir? What about Mr. Hakimi?"

"I was never keen on the man from the beginning, Ram. But I had no choice at the time. I know he was not well-liked by the workers and his manner was rude and disrespectful." The man grimaced and exhaled in frustration. "I also understand, now, that he was responsible for the dismissal of your friend, Sudi, from back in Nepal. I am very sorry. It is one of the biggest errors in judgement I have made since forming this company. I found out this week that Mr. Hakimi was cutting corners on the quality of our building materials and pocketing the money. I fired him myself just today and he is now being prosecuted for his crimes against the company."

Ram nodded, but his brain spun with the news. He had known there was something not quite right about the man, but he would never have guessed that his character was this low.

"Have you spoken to your friend, Sudi, since he left?"

"No, sir. All I know is that he is up in Cairo, working now. We have not spoken since he left…it was so sudden and all. I hope to see him during the festival."

"I see. If you do see him, please give him my apologies and let him know he is more than welcome to return here, if he so desires."

"Of course, sir. It would be my pleasure."

"So, do we have a deal, Ram?"

"Yes, sir, we do. I will not let you down."

"I know you won't. Thank you, Ram, and have a good time. My best wishes to your new wife, as well."

Ram grasped the man's large hand in both of his and shook it enthusiastically, then stood and took his leave. It was incredible! Not only could he go home to see Priya and his parents again, but when he returned, he would be in a position of real authority. He and Mereruka would be working side by side as supervisors in the field. Not only that, but it meant even more money.

Ram was sure he was walking home that night, but it was like his feet never touched the ground. He was just so elated. He cleaned up from work and ran over to Mereruka's home to share the good news. His friend seemed more thrilled than Ram and insisted they go out to celebrate.

And celebrate, they did.

18.

Big News

After two more weeks, Ram found himself back on a transport to Nepal. He could not wait to share the news with his family.

He burst from the cart that dropped him off at Chandisthan and met Priya midway across the village square. She hugged him tightly. It was like no other feeling that Ram had ever known. The months apart had felt like an eternity; he could not believe he was holding her again.

They walked across the square, arm in arm. Ram saw his father sitting alone outside the house in his favorite spot, his hands clasped firmly over the top of the walking stick that Ram had given him.

He stood shakily and greeted his son, calling for his wife to join them. Ram turned as his mother hurried through the door and hugged him warmly. It was good to see them, but even in the few months he had been away, he could see they were aging rapidly.

His mother was still quite mobile, but his father now could only walk with heavy reliance on the walking stick. His mother, though walking with ease, was pale and drawn in her face. Ram sighed. It was a pain in Ram's heart to see, but he knew he could take over as the family's means of support, especially with his new position.

They went inside as the sun set and shared a meal. Ram saw that it was now Priya who was taking on this chore. It was his mother's recipes, for sure, but his wife was now the one doing the cooking. Ram supposed that the intervening months since the wedding had been filled with Priya learning the family cuisine and other household chores.

She looked radiant as she bustled about, taking care of everything. Ram felt guilty as he watched, but what he knew of Priya made him realize she had just stepped up and done what was necessary. He would speak to her later to see what he could do to help her with this adjustment.

They retired as usual to the living area and Ram was the one now to light the fire. He listened with care as his parents filled him in on what had happened in Chandisthan since he left. Adarsh, they said, was now tending the fields and small herd of goats that his father once had taken care of. He was, his mother said, doing well, though she suspected he missed his old job in Egypt.

"Farming just does not seem to be in Adarsh's blood, Ram. He does it because he has to take care of his mother and two sisters. But he just looks sad and lost sometimes. You should visit him while you are here."

"Of course, mother. He was instrumental in me getting the job in Samalout. I miss not seeing him every day. And how is Nirijan?"

His mother looked away into the fire and did not reply right away.

"Mother?"

"Oh, Ram...I do not even know how to tell you. I guess you should just hear the truth."

Ram felt his heart sink.

"Nirijan was on his way back here after his injury in Egypt. He was in Kathmandu, waiting for a transport home. From what we were told, he was misidentified as a government rebel of some sort by the Maoist soldiers that are everywhere in Kathmandu now."

"Soldiers?"

"Oh, yes. This is probably new to you, as well. Maoist forces from China have spilt over into Nepal now as an extension of their insistence on retaking Tibet. The Dalai Lama has fled and they are running roughshod over everyone now. We hear there are armed soldiers on every corner in Kathmandu and travelers all have to produce proper identification papers all along the trekking trails now. In the Everest region, as well as here up in the Annapurnas. It is terribly sad."

Ram could hardly believe his ears. It was heart-breaking to hear, knowing the peaceful Nepalis were now being targeted by the Chinese. He felt a deep despair fall over him, and he was glad he had long ago departed Kathmandu. He hoped the Kadys were still safe.

"Oh, mother…so, what of Nirijan?"

"As I said, he was just waiting for a transport back here. He was limping badly and one of the soldiers alerted the others that he was a government spy wanted in China. Nirijan was startled by the sudden accusation, and turned to explain that they had his confused with someone else. He reached into his pocket to show his identification."

"Oh, no, mother…"

"I am sorry, Ram. They told the police he was reaching for a gun and they had to defend themselves."

"A gun? Nirijan?"

"Yes. It was all lies. This is life in Nepal now, Ram."

Ram felt like his heart was breaking. Two of his best friends from Chandisthan were lost to him, and the third had been forced into a life he hated. He was hoping that Sudi was home for the festival so he could pass along the owner's apologies at least.

Nirijan was dead. It seemed like a nightmare. *How could this have happened?* He sat silently, tears in his eyes as he stared through the flames. He had wanted to surprise everyone with his good news, but now just did not seem like the right moment.

He helped Priya get his parents to bed, then retired with her as well.

"Are you all right, Ram?"

Priya pulled herself close to Ram as they got into bed.

"I suppose so. This news just came as a shock."

He filled her in on what had happened to Sudi and how he hoped to find him at the festival and possibly bring him back to Samalout when he returned.

"Have you seen him yet?"

"No. Not yet. Maybe he is on his way?"

"Perhaps. I had big news for everyone, but after what I just heard, it did not seem like the right time for it."

"Big news?"

Ram turned to face Priya and he explained what had led to his being able to come back for the festival and his new promotion upon his return.

"My God, Ram. That is wonderful!"

"It is. I still cannot believe it myself."

"You are not the only one with big news, my husband."

"Oh?"

"I am pregnant."

19.

Good Fortune

Ram felt all the breath go out of him.

"Pregnant? You are sure?"

"Yes. I am sure."

Ram felt his emotions flip in the few seconds it taken Priya to tell him. All the turmoil and despair that had filled his mind was instantly erased. He hugged Priya tightly and felt a sense of love and happiness fill him that he had never imagined possible.

"When did you find out?"

"After you left to go back to Egypt. All the signs were there, so I got my father to take me to a doctor for a test to make sure."

"Do you know if it's a boy or a girl?"

"I do not know. There is no one close that can do that test, and they said it was too early to know for sure, anyway."

"But I know someone who can."

Priya looked at him oddly. "You mean that psychic up near Khudi Bazaar?"

"Yes. She is almost always right. We should go up in the next day or so. She will tell us."

"Can we afford that? I hear she is very expensive."

"With my new job in Egypt, I am sure it will be no problem. Priya, this is fantastic!"

The next morning, Ram sat with his parents and filled them in on his new job. He was sure they were happy for him, but it was not apparent that they truly understood the huge opportunity that had been given to him. They were more excited and thrilled with the fact that they would soon be grandparents. Ram just laughed to himself.

Priya had told him of his parents' rapidly failing health that morning, but that she was more than happy to be able to take care of them in his absence. Her own mother was coming by from time to time to help, as well, so it was no problem.

Ram and Priya did not tell anyone else in Chandisthan about their plans to consult the psychic up in Khudi Bazaar. A lot of the locals still saw this type of thing as black magic, making a mockery of their Buddhist or Hindu faiths. The woman was scorned by many. Also, there were few, if any, around who could have afforded her services even if they believed in her purported abilities.

Ram and Priya began the short, steep hike up the trail to find her just before noon. They moved slowly and talked as they went. Ram did not want to put any extra strain on Priya than was necessary. If he could have done this without her having to be physically present, he would have, but he knew that the pregnant mother needed to be there.

Ram never told Priya, but he was secretly hoping for a son. He would love the child no matter what, but he was praying for a son.

They crested the ridge shortly and Ram had Priya sit at the tea house where he had met often with Roger Garrison while he went in search of the psychic. He was sure he would not be there, but Ram could not help looking around the area for Roger. There were lots of Western visitors, but none looked even remotely like his friend from Oregon in America. Ram laughed at himself for even considering such a thing.

He left the tea house and wandered along the path that went beside a short stone wall, farther up the hill behind where he had left Priya. A man outside had directed Ram to where the psychic lived and he stared at the run-down hovel with hesitation. The path ran out and Ram found himself wading through bushes to reach the door of the hut.

He knocked tentatively and obeyed a disembodied-sounding voice to enter. He pushed open the splintered door, which creaked loudly on hinges that seemed as if they had not been attended to in years.

The interior of the hut was lit only by a single candle on a table across the one-room structure. All the windows were caked over from age and a brownish debris that Ram had no interest in figuring out the source of. The candle flickered as if blown by a breeze, even though the day was still and there was no apparent source of wind anywhere.

"Close the door, my friend. You are letting the spirits out." A shrill voice cackled in laughter.

Ram froze at the sound of the high-pitched voice. It came from across the room, but seemed as if it came from all around him, as well. He forced the stubborn door closed and the candle continued to waver anyway. Ram squinted his eyes, letting them adjust to the darkness of the room, but he could not see anyone.

"You have come for your wife?"

Ram looked again, trying to locate the source of the voice, but it was in vain. It seemed at once to be in front of him, behind him, and over him.

"I have, ma'am."

"Step closer so I can get a read on you, my friend."

The voice had fallen in pitch a bit and now did seem to be coming from just to his left. Ram turned his head and saw a woman so frail and pale that he might have been able to see right through her, if not for the dark cloak she wore like a shroud.

Ram felt a twinge of fear, but something inside him told him to go ahead; it was safe. The woman's face was mostly concealed by the hood of her garment, but as Ram came closer, the candle illuminated her features. She eased the hood back so he could see her.

She let the hood fall away and smiled at Ram. The odd voice and even odder attire did not fit with the woman's appearance. She was indeed pale and very thin, but her skin was young and rosy. A mane of thick blonde hair fell down her back, the bulk of it gathered in a mass just behind her head. Her eyes were a brilliant blue and they peered deeply at Ram as if they could read him intimately.

"Can I have your hand, my friend?"

Ram was not sure why, but without any hesitation or reservation, he offered the woman his hand. She turned it so his palm was facing up and ran her long index finger along the various lines on his palm. She closed her eyes and was immobile and silent as she held his hand, as if in a trance of some sort.

"You have come to determine the sex of your unborn child, yes?"

"We have, ma'am."

"And your wife? She is with you?"

"At the tea house, just down the path."

"Is she able to walk up here?"

"Yes. I wanted to find you first, then bring her once I knew you were here."

"Certainly, my friend. Fetch her at once and we can begin. It will allow me time to prepare."

She released Ram's hand and he backed away slowly, beginning to wonder what he had stepped into. He left the hut and found Priya just where he had left her, sipping on tea. She smiled as he came in.

"You found her?"

"Um...I did. She is odd, but she already knew why we were here before I said anything."

Priya just shrugged. Ram helped her up and led her back to the woman's hut. They entered and the woman indicated that Priya should sit at the table directly across from her. Ram stood directly behind Priya and waited to see what might happen next.

The woman closed her eyes again and asked Priya for her hand this time. Ram watched as she performed the same ritual with Priya as she had with him.

"So, Priya…how long have you been pregnant?"

Ram felt his blood run cold as the woman, without any introduction, had known Priya's name.

"About two or three months now, I think."

"And you want to know if you are to have a boy or a girl, is that correct?"

"It is. Yes."

The woman released her hand and rose gracefully from her seat at the table. She moved to Priya's side of the table, appearing as if she floated, rather than walked. There were no sounds to her movement until she came to a spot near Priya and took a deep breath. She knelt in front of Priya and stretched her fingers wide before gently placing them across her belly. She made no sounds or movements for a few minutes.

Ram was beginning to worry when the woman removed her hands, stood, and floated back to her original chair. She replaced the hood of her cloak on her head and smiled at the waiting couple.

"Ram, Priya…congratulations. You are soon to be the proud parents of a new baby boy. Ram? Your desires for a son are to be fulfilled."

It was simple and definitive. There was no more said. Ram handed the woman some rupees and they began to make their way out of her presence and back to the tea house. They had just reached the door, when the woman called out.

"And Ram…take care in this new job of yours. Your wife and your new son need you."

"Of course, ma'am. Thank you."

With that, the woman seemed to just meld into the shadows and the candle blew out, though neither Ram nor Priya had felt a breeze that might have done so. They closed her door and went back to the tea house to talk. Ram brought them both a warm chai and they sat at a small table that overlooked the trails that led to the upper reaches of the mountains above.

Neither spoke for a few minutes, then Priya broke the silence.

"Did you tell her my name before you took me up there?"

"No. In fact, I never told her my name, either. She just knew."

"Really?"

Ram nodded and sipped his tea.

"When I first went up there, she took my hand just like she took yours. She held it and then she knew why we were here, just like that. I never said a word."

"Maybe someone in the village told her before we arrived?"

"Perhaps, but I did not get that feeling. Did you?"

"No, I guess not."

"And anyway, how did she know our names without us telling her? And she knew about my new position with the company in Egypt. I never said anything."

Priya stopped mid-sip and a look of wonder passed over her face.

"Ram? Can I ask you a question?"

"Yes."

"She said your desires for a son were to be fulfilled. Have you been wishing for a son?"

Ram felt his ears redden. The comment from the woman had slipped by him in all the weirdness that had transpired in the hut.

"I have. It is not like I would not welcome a daughter and love her with all my heart. But if I am honest? Yes. I had been hoping for a son."

"That is okay. I was just curious. This was a most unusual experience, yes?"

Ram nodded in agreement and laughed along with Priya as they finished their drinks and headed back down the hill. They were in love! Ram thought his hard work was finally paying off. His fortune must be turning.

20.

The Middle Way

Sudi never did appear in Chandisthan for the festival that fall. So now, Ram was faced with one of his friends being most likely somewhere in Cairo, while Nirijan was dead and Adarsh was miserable.

He had gone to see Adarsh as his mother had suggested, but it had been an uncomfortable and awkward visit. Ram had tried to remain as upbeat and positive as he could, but the negative aura that was flowing off Adarsh was more than Ram could stand. He had not had anything to do with Adarsh's run of bad luck, but it seemed like his friend was angry at him because he was doing so well and Adarsh was not.

Ram stayed as long as he could, but he began to feel that he was making Adarsh's situation worse by just coming to see him. He left his friend's house feeling bad for Adarsh, but Ram had no idea what to do to make it any better for him. He briefly thought of offering him some money, but then, he recalled how proud and self-reliant the old Adarsh had been. He was sure it would have made him even angrier. Deep inside Adarsh was might even have been jealous of Ram's life.

He went home sad, but as soon as he saw Priya with his parents, Ram felt his spirits lift. He had tried. That was all he could do. They had a delightful dinner together, enjoying a concoction that Priya had come up with on her own from a basic recipe from her mother-in-law. Ram could detect the tell-tale unique curry from his mother, but whatever Priya had used to adapt it had improved it immeasurably. Ram never thought he would say that about his mother's cooking.

"The curry was so good, I could not stop eating. Did you use any special ingredients tonight?" Ram asked.

Priya glanced up and gave Ram a brief smile and said, " No, it is the same as usual. May be you were hungrier than normal."

"Huh" Ram said with his mouth full of rice and curry. After a short pause, he looked at Priya again and mumbled, "My hunger was the same. I think the special ingredient is your love." Even with the mumble, Priya heard him loud and clear. She was now blushing and could not even look at Ram.

It was a wonderful evening and Ram was trying to hold onto the feeling as long as he could. He loved seeing Priya blush and smile. He loved the look she gave him anytime he teased her. The look that said, I love you but don't tease me around the in-laws. The look that showed how much in love they were. There was nothing he would rather be doing than to stay close to his beloved wife, looking into her eyes and holding her in his arms. He was engulfed in the emotion more than every today. He was trying to cherish every second he could spend with Priya. Ram always wondered how he got so lucky to deserve a wife like Priya. With her, he had experienced emotions he did not knew existed.

The next morning, he was due to make the trek back to Kathmandu, then overland to Samalout. The day dawned long before Ram would have preferred it to.

He lingered in the addition with Priya as long as he could before having to pack up and go back to work. The trip, as usual, had been delightful, but leaving now was doubly hard after having found out that he was to be a father. He got butterflies in his stomach every time he thought about this. He wondered how the kid would look like. Ram would have loved to stay home and take are of his wife. Ram wanted to be there to see his wife's glowing face and to feel his son kick and turn in his wife's belly. More than ever Ram wanted to be with his family. He also knew though everything he was doing was for his family. He wanted to take care of his parents and make sure that Priya and his son were always taken care of. He knew all this sacrifice would be well worth it one day.

If not for the situation with his parents, Ram would have arranged for Priya to join him in Egypt. She was still not so far along in her pregnancy that she could not have made the trip. Also, Ram was sure he would have had no difficulty in finding them their own place in Samalout.

But with the health of his parents on the steady decline, that was not even an option. Between Priya and her parents' help, Ram was counting on them to take care of his parents' physical needs while he took care of them financially.

He repeated the same depressing routine of farewells he had in the past, knowing that this time, it might be another year before he was able to come back to Nepal. His new job was apt to have more responsibilities that might preclude the twice-yearly excursions back home. He was sure, though, that he might be able to talk his way into being home for the birth of his son.

He walked over to his parents, touched their feet with his hand to get their blessings. Then, he walked over to Priya, held her tight and gave her a kiss on her forehead. Ram then got on his knees, put his hand around Priya's belly and started talking to his son.

" Hey little man, I will not be around much as you are growing in there. I am working hard to make sure you have the best life possible. I want to be here right with you and your mom when you open your eyes to the world." Ram said with a cracking voice. As always, Ram was trying his best not to cry. Ram continued "Babu, when I come back, I hope you remember my voice from these couple weeks. Your mom makes the best food in this world, so I know you are happy and relaxed in there. Don't give her too much trouble. I will be here to hold you before you know." Ram wiped off his tears before anyone could see him, kissed his wife's belly and got up swiftly to leave.

His bags were finally loaded and he begrudgingly set off. The only saving grace that Ram had now was that this new job would allow him to more fully provide for everyone he loved.

The return trip was uneventful. Ram was soon back on the job site in Samalout, but now as a supervisor alongside Mereruka. It was not as physically taxing as his old position had been, but he was responsible for a team of workers now, not just himself. However, the fact that he was well-liked and respected among his team made the daily routine more palatable.

His team knew him well and, despite his young age, they responded well to his direction and leadership. As a group, they had abhorred Hakimi. They found Ram's helpful, kind style of leadership infinitely more enjoyable than the former foreman's way. New projects were coming into them regularly, and the workflow was going as smoothly as anyone in recent memory could recall.

Ram was enjoying his new role and found that the owner was extremely pleased, too. What was now on in Ram's mind most of all – besides the details of his work – was his son. When he got off work or had breaks, all Ram could think about was what to name him and how he was going to give him everything he could. All the things that his own father had been unable to provide to Ram would now be there for his son.

It was, he realized, the desire of each successive generation to want more for their children. He had already seen that clearly when his parents had set him up for an education in Kathmandu.

But that arrangement had not been without its downsides. It had been the only option his parents had. Ram wanted to make sure his son did not have to endure the trials that he had gone through.

The one thought that kept coming back to haunt him, though, was that being away so much was not fair. Not to his son, not to Priya, not to himself. He was sure there must be a way to resolve that dilemma and still make sure his parents were taken care of as they aged. Like always, Ram made a mental note to redirect his meditations to address this. In all his life, this had never failed to offer him solutions to his problems, and he was sure it could give him answers here, as well.

Ram knew that working as hard as he could here would provide all the good things that his son should have: adequate food and shelter, a good education, nice clothes, and a long and healthy life. That was not a problem. Ram was not afraid of hard work.

What nagged at him was not being around to see his son grow up. That had been one thing that he so treasured about the relationship he had experienced with his father. They had not always had enough to eat and the house was sometimes in need of repairs they could not afford, but he had loved being around his father when he was young. Somewhere, there had to be a middle ground – as the Buddha had spoken of, "The Middle Way".

Ram tried to craft his own Middle Way by increasing his workload more than ever before. There was no limit to the hours he could work, so he forged away, often long into the night. Perhaps if he worked extra hard, he could earn more money and more praise from his boss. Then, if he requested leave to go home and visit his soon-to-be-born son, his boss might not object.

The additional work was more strenuous than Ram had anticipated. His muscles ached and no amount of rest stopped him from feeling perpetually tired. The Egyptian heat was brutal, as always, but Ram knew he could handle it. He was a hard worker, after all. Nothing could hold him back from providing for his family.

The rest of the workers on Ram's team had already left the site for their mid-day break, but Ram stayed behind. He could not afford a break; the work needed to be done, and the sooner he finished it, the sooner he could return to his wife and son.

The sun was at the highest point in the sky, beating down on Ram's back without mercy. He wiped sweat from his eyes as he looked across the job site. There was so much left to do, but he had to finish it. Tools in hand, he continued, determination coursing through him.

Some of the other workers called for him to join them, but he shook his head and carried on. He had to set an example for them, too. How was he to expect his team to work hard if their own foreman wasn't working hard with them? No, he could not stop.

"Ram, you need water!" someone called out. "It's too hot out here!"

"I'm fine," he called back. "Let me just do this last bit. It's almost done."

The worker shrugged and rejoined the others, casting wary glances his way. He paid them no mind. This was his Middle Way, the middle ground he had been looking for. He could work hard to provide for his family and be there for them when they needed him. All would be well. After all, Ram was no stranger to manual labor.

His weariness grew quickly, until Ram could barely hold onto the tools he gripped in his wet palms. He looked up at the sun, so bright and hot above him that it blurred his vision. Maybe he did need some water.

No, he couldn't stop. If he rested, even for just a moment, he feared he would not have the strength to keep working. He gritted his teeth and went back to work.

Just a little more, he thought to himself, for my son.

21.

Loyalty

Back in Chandisthan, Priya was getting closer and closer to giving birth to their son. They had sent many telegrams and other messages to Ram in Samalout, but there had been no responses. This was not like Ram, Priya knew. He had always been responsive to letters and telegrams in the past. Maybe they were not even reaching him.

Maybe the Maoists were screening and censoring communications and not allowing mail to go through. She had heard the situation in Kathmandu was growing progressively worse. Egypt was such a long way off. The post office in Kathmandu was also notorious for opening international mail, hoping for cash. There had been numerous times when she had received her letter already opened.

There were so many things that could be the cause. She knew it had to be one of these. Ram would not just ignore them.

More weeks passed, and still nothing arrived back in Chandisthan from Ram. Priya was beginning to get very worried. They had sent multiple messages informing him of the rapidly approaching birth of his son. Could it be that his company was blocking his mail? It seemed a long shot to Priya, as Ram had always spoken so highly of them and with such admiration and respect.

It was still a possibility, though. She had heard of many companies that withheld mail and worse, kept the workers from leaving by withholding their passport. Maybe things had changed with the company. She had heard bad stories of the kefala that existed in the Middle East from Nepali migrant workers. Ram had assured her that this was not the case with his company, though. It was just hard not knowing.

Priya had heard of many men who had abandoned their families after they started getting settled abroad. Being away from family a year at a time had been difficult for these men and they ended up marrying a local woman. Priya had never doubted Ram's loyalty, but now, she did not know what to think. Was he loyal to her? His work? Or, something – or someone – else entirely?

Human instinct is an interesting thing, they come out of nowhere but is good at leaving this uncomfortable feeling deep inside you. Priya had been getting this feeling for a while now. In her heart, she felt like something is wrong, but had nothing that she could point to.

Ram's parents were now very weak and his mother was suffering from hallucinations and visions. She had convinced herself that something awful had happened to Ram. She spent hours in the house, rocking herself back and forth, crying and wailing in anguish. It was more than Priya could take, some days.

Ram's father was weak, physically, but was mentally strong as ever. He kept telling his wife and Priya that Ram was probably just too busy to reply.

"You two have too much time on your hands to sit around and worry all day. Ram is working and does not have time to write to you all the time," he would say. "He will probably just show up one of these days," Baba added.

Not too long after, Priya had her baby in Chandisthan. It was, as the psychic had predicted, a son, thus making Ram's dreams for a son realized. He was healthy and had a nice combination of both Ram and Priya's features. The birth had gone well. Priya had been brave all throughout the many hours of labor. She had prayed each day that Ram would come bursting through the door, but he never did.

The birth of their grandchild brought new life to Ram's parents, as well. They spent their days playing with and taking care of the newborn.

Ram's mother would invite villagers passing by their house to come over and bless the baby. It seemed like there were always visitors in the house now. It was as if the festivals had come early this year.

Priya had been dreaming of when Ram arrived home. He would be so excited to hold his baby, and so proud that it's a boy. She hoped that he could stay home and start a business with the money he had saved. Then, he wouldn't have to leave her and their son ever again.

*****

It was a warm Saturday morning and Priya and her mother-in-law were sitting in the front porch, putting oil on the baby. He loved when they gave him oil massage. All the woman in the village had told her how the oil makes the baby's skin stronger.

The Himalayas in the backdrop of Chandisthan were crystal-clear today. The peaks looked gorgeous, with just a few clouds floating around them. It was very peaceful; Priya thought it must be a sign of a good day.

There was a faint sound of a vehicle far away in the village. Priya wondered for a second if Ram had decided to surprise them and come back without any notice. Then again, she knew Ram always walked home after he got off the bus. It could not be him, even if he was going to surprise them.

The noise from the vehicle got louder and village kids were running after it, just like they had when the Kadys came to pick up Ram years ago. Priya ignored the noise, thinking it was probably just going to a different house. But as the noise got closer and closer to her house, her emotions were on a roller coaster.

Did Ram really show up unannounced?

What if it was the Kadys coming to look for Ram? Could he get in trouble for leaving his employment in Kathmandu abruptly?

The truck finally stopped close to their house, and it was no ordinary Land Rover. It was an ambulance.

She was confused. Everyone in her house was completely healthy.

Before she could play any scenarios in her head, two men wearing white coats got out of the truck. They opened the back and took out a large wooden box. They walked toward her solemnly, carrying the shiny coffin.

At last, Ram was home.

Author's Note

Thank you for making it to the end of the book.

Dreams from Nepal was a story of those who could not write their own. It was a story of those who never gave up hope. Many of you are probably thinking Ram did not deserve this ending. Ram worked so hard, and had been through so much in life. He did everything he was supposed to. This should not be his fate. I agree with you 100%. No, this absolutely should not be his fate!

My goal with *Dreams from Nepal* was to capture some of the difficult realities of families in remote Nepal. It is heart wrenching to think about the choices a parent has to make in hopes of good life for their children. These innocent children who go to the cities gleaming with hope of better life are often disappointed with the fate that awaits them. This work of fiction is not far from the real life of many poor families. Over 500,00 Nepali youth leave home every year in search of better opportunities. Most of them working in the gulf countries, do not always have the best working and living conditions. What is worse is the alarming number of people who end up having the same fate as Ram's. According to Associated Press analysis of data released by Nepal's ministry of labor and employment, one out of every five hundred Nepali who started this journey in 2015 returned home in a coffin.

So, the abrupt ending is on purpose. Life is abrupt, even when it seems normal. Unfortunately, this is a sad reality for thousands of youths in Nepal and other developing countries alike. Young men leave their family and hometown in hopes of creating a better life for themselves and their families. They have dreams of a better life, a better tomorrow and many of those dreams turn into casket of dreams.

Thanks for your support!

Love,

Bikul Koirala

Glossary

Bagh Chal – A strategic, two-player board game that originated in Nepal. The game is asymmetric in that one player controls four tigers and the other player controls up to twenty goats. The tigers "hunt" the goats while the goats attempt to block the tigers' movements.

Betel – A type of palm nut.

Camphor – A waxy, flammable substance used in Hindu religious ceremonies.

Diwali – Diwali, or Deepavali, is the Hindu festival of lights, celebrated every year in autumn.

Doko – A V-shaped bamboo basket used to carry goods in Nepal.

Falafel – Deep-fried balls made of ground chickpeas or fava beans.

Fuul – An Egyptian breakfast of fava beans with Tahini.

Goddhuwa – A part of the ritual in Hindu weddings where the relatives wash the feet of the bride and groom.

Guptaghar – Literal meaning is "secret house"; usually the room set up for the bride and groom to spend their first night together in.

Janti – A wedding procession in Hindu culture, where the groom and his family go to the bride's home to pick her up.

Kalash – A small metallic pitcher used in Hindu rituals.

Kanyadaan – A ritual in Hindu weddings when the bride's father and family give her to the groom.

Kefala – A system used to monitor migrant laborers, working primarily in the construction and domestic sectors in Lebanon, Bahrain, Iraq, Jordan, Kuwait, Oman, Qatar, Saudi Arabia, and the UAE.

Lassis – A sweet drink made with yoghurt and water, often flavored with seasonal fruits.

Mahseer – A type of fish found in the Himalayan region.

Mandap – A stage setup for the wedding ceremony

Namaste – A respectful form of greeting in Hindu custom; a common form of greeting in Nepal.

Pallanguli – A board game of Indian origin, popular among children and the elderly.

Pida – A wooden seat that is barely above the ground level.

Pote – A type of colorful, beaded necklace.

Sherpas – People with the last name "Sherpa"; an ethnic group from the most mountainous regions of Nepal.

Sindhoor – Vermillion red powder, commonly worn by married Hindu women between their parted hair.

Ta'amiya – An Egyptian dish very similar to falafel.

Tika – A red mark used in Hindu culture as a form of blessing.

Topi – A type of Nepali hat, made of fabric and worn as a symbol of national pride.

About the Author

Bikul Koirala is an entrepreneur and author of the emotional novel, *Dreams from Nepal*. Born and raised in Nepal, Koirala set out to be a chemist, but soon found the courage and motivation to pursue his more creative calling. Now, he designs mobile apps, hosts a professional blog, and writes about what inspires him. Through the power of storytelling, Koirala writes about culture, humanity, technology, education, and unique perspectives. *Dreams from Nepal* is his first venture into fictional literature.

Koirala lives in Fort Collins, Colorado with his family and dog. He enjoys the great outdoors, craft beer, and reading anything he can get his hands on.

Learn more and contact him at www.bikul.net.

Made in the USA
Middletown, DE
21 January 2018